AF443007

GH
Guildford
PUBLISHING

SHATTERED
A ROMANCE BUILT ON LIES & DECEIT
JC PIPKIN

SHATTERED

A ROMANCE BUILT ON LIES & DECEIT

JC PIPKIN

ISBN-13: 9798723092600

ACKNOWLEDGEMENTS

First & Foremost, I would like to thank God for given me the opportunity share the precious gift of writing with others.

I would like to thank Marenda of Kingsandqueens publication for believing in me and giving the chance to tell my stories.

Also, I would like to thank my wife Dah-ziana Moore for supporting my dreams and standing by my side all the way. And I would like to thank all the people that supported me along the way.

Thank You!

DEDICATION

This book is dedicated to all the women that struggle with the insecurities society placed on them. Love yourself first and the rest will definitely follow. Don't ever let anyone define who you are, because your imperfections are what makes you perfect!!!!

SLEEP IN PEACE

STATEN ISLAND, NEW YORK

Niekia "Keda" Williams, Boyce "Beanie" Kelly, Clayton Lewis, Steven "Rock" Pipkin, Shane kelly. Najea Smith, Prince "Wuda" Edmonds, Cedric "Ced" Black.

Clarrise Lewis, Barry blue, Mike Kelly, Sandy Brock. Ricardo "Ricky B" Bell, Moleik Beverly, Jermaine "Big Den" Dickerson, Garland "SI" Tyree, June June(God Inf), Big Sincere, Ozzie Linwood, Michael "Cee-Born" Haynie, June Bug, Alafia "Laf" Rodriquez, Ana Desousa, Damon "Coo-Coo Dame" Henderson, The God Water, Big Bar, Jam, Kyre "Hound" Henderson, Kameek "Lil Meek" Sears, Eric Gardner, Big Gee, Vincent "Tinker" Graham Jr, Avanti "Bt" Brock.

WILMINGTON, DELAWARE

Keshell "KeKe" Anderson, Michelle "Bird" Moore, Bobby Dimes, Jerome "Bam Bam" Mcdole, Tommier "Mierzy" Dendy, Damar Smith, Shareef Hamilton, Kayveon Mcgriff, Raquan Davis, Eddie Green, Micheal Reams, William "Lil Bill" Rollins, Jordan Ellerbe, Brandon Wingo, Tyreek Scott, Kaden Young, Yaseem "Sosa" Powell, Tynesia Cephas, Latrice "Peaches" Blackshear, Ryjee Pinkney, Michael Parker, Calvin Peterson, Purnell Green, Shaun Purvis, Jaiwon Pollard, Mellow.

Here, I lie upon the shores under a broken sky...

Cast away, forgotten!

How can thy love simply fade away? No
goodbye, no kiss, nor thy hand a simple wave?

Inside of my heart the walls are now
darkened and gray...

No more smiles, no more joy,
not even laughter laughs and play.

-JC PIPKIN

CHAPTER 1

Miracle awoke to an empty and cold bed. A quiet stillness filled the room as she stretched and yawned. There was a heavy sadness in the silence, a loneliness, that had become her steady companion over the past couple of years. Her love life was nonexistent and she became accustom to hearing the steady beat of her own heart, instead of the sound of two hearts beating together as one. She was desperate for the affections of a man and the chance to reciprocate those affections in return, because she knew she had a whole heart filled with love to give. But in reality, there seemed to be no one interested in accepting the love she had to offer. Miracle sighed and snatched away the silky sheets that covered her nakedness as she slid her thick legs over the edge of the queen sized bed. *Another loveless ass day.* She bemoaned, tentatively placing her manicured feet on the carpeted floor and grudgingly stood erect.

She hated waking up in the mornings, especially alone, and horny. She was tempted to crawl back into bed and cuddle up with her faithful dildo, Mr. Long-stroke, as the weakness between her legs urged her to do so. *Damn! A bitch seriously need some dick in her life.* She thought, trying to ignore the nagging voice of her own kitty as she fought back the temptation raging through her. But the saddest part about it, she couldn't even remember the last time she had some good dick inside of her. It was pathetic and embarrassing to admit. But in truth, she was tired of pleasing herself and longed for a nigga to service her every whim and need. She was beyond sexually frustrated. She was at the point in her life where she would even settle for a one night stand. To her, service was service, even a single's night of pleasure with some strange dick beat a blank any lonely day. But even that, solely depended on what kind of meal a man happened to have a taste for, because most of the men she came across only seemed interested in nibbling on a saucer of sushi, not a hefty dish of steak and potato's and she was definitely more than a mouthful to swallow.

She shrugged off the thoughts of her pathetic sex life and shuffled down the hallway to the bathroom and brushed the foulness out of her mouth, then stood back and stared hard at her reflection in the mirror. A beautiful round, dark-chocolate face stared back at her with silky jet-black flowing hair. It was a beautiful image. But to her, it wasn't the image she saw in the mirror, only the ugliness of a lifetime of rejection and she couldn't see the true beauty through her own eyes. She was blinded by the opinions of others, instead of being influenced by her own self-worth. Her entire life had been surrounded with ridicule, especially growing up in the Foster Care system. She was constantly picked on outside; in school, in playgrounds, and the pool. But the cafeteria at school was even worse. It was like the opening season at a gun range, and she was the primary target. Other student's would clown her about how she looked in the tight form-fitting clothes she wore and being over weight, dressed in a too-small track suit, made it even more humiliating.

God, why can't I find a man that's gonna love me for me? And accept me for who I am? She thought, feeling the sharp claws of dejection digging deep at her soul. She hated the way she looked, short and round. It was a heavy burden to bear, a two-hundred and fifty pound burden, and being five-foot-five only made matters worse. *Pleasurably plump!* She scoffed to herself. *Who the fuck came up with that saying? There was nothing pleasurable about being fat.* She thought as she stared at her voluptuous reflection in the mirror. Her sad light-brown eyes reflected the pain and loneliness that came from being over weight in all the wrong places. Through-out the 29 years of her existence, she had secretly struggled with the insecurity of being over weight and feeling as though she was worthless. Unlovable. But to those around her, they were unaware of her low self-esteem issues, because she learned well to conceal that part of herself from others. To them, she was ever the out-going person; extremely bright and witty with a personality that could brighten the gloomiest day. But deep inside, she was unable to hide the truth from herself.

Miracle loved and craved food. It was an addiction spawned long ago by rejection. Taking priority in her life over most things an average woman would desire. Food to her, was the same fix as Heroine was to a dope sick junkie, she had to have it. And If given a choice? She would choose food over some good dick hands down. Therefore, it was the cause of many lonely nights without a man. Even on those rare occasions when she tried to find a decent man to date, it seemed impossible, because most of the men she desired were to busy chasing after something she didn't have...A perfect figure. It was depressing and miserable, leaving food as her only resort and constant companion. She felt as though no none understood what she was going through and hated when people were quick to say; *"There's somebody out there for everyone."* If that was so, then where was her someone at? Because he definitely wasn't hiding in her cabinets. *Lying mother fuckers!* She thought, shaking her head.

Miracle reluctantly tore herself away from the mirror and climbed under the hot spraying water in the shower and tried scrubbing away the self loathing that stubbornly clung to her body and watched as it pooled down the drain at her feet. Swirling into an unknown oblivion. It was at those moments, alone in the shower, that she desperately wished she could scrub away the extra pounds as easily as she washed the dirt off her body. But so much for wishful thinking. After showering and toweling off, she shuffled back to the loneliness of her bedroom, where even the pink colored walls held a shade of loneliness to them. She plopped her large frame down onto the bed and wondered if she should bother getting dressed or sashay her nakedness around the house. She chose the latter. Besides, there wasn't nobody around to see her in full voluptuous form.

As she started lathering down her body, with the fragrant smell of 'Warm Vanilla Sugar' lotion, which was her signature scent, her phone rang and she quickly reached for it on the nightstand table and answered it.

"Hello?"

"Morning bitch!" It was her best friend Heaven. "I hope your ready for tonight. Because your ass is going out with me and I'm not letting you chicken out on a bitch." Heaven said teasingly, because the last time they had planned a night out Miracle reneged at the last moment.

"Damn! A bitch just woke up and got out of the shower. Can I at least lotion my ass and get something to eat? You know a bitch can't function without food." Miracle shot back as she put the phone on speaker so she could properly finish lathering down her body. As a big woman, She had to make sure she didn't miss an inch as she got deep inside the crevice of her stomach. *A bitch definitely can't forget to get under there!* She thought to herself mindfully.

"That's all your greedy ass wanna do is eat." Heaven joked, even though her words was laced with the truth.

"I'm a fat bitch, what you expect. I can't be skipping meals like you skinny bitches." Miracle countered and they both laughed. Heaven had a high pitch laughter and it sounded shrill through the phone's speaker.

"You need to be cooking up a dick to suck on." She laughed.

"I bet a bitch could put together one hell of nigga too. A bitch gonna have to go through her cook book." Miracle conceptualized with a laugh as she placed the lotion back among her ever growing collection of Bath & Body Works and fished through her drawer and picked out a sexy pink-colored Veronica Ann pantie set. "So what time are you coming to pick me up?" She asked, squeezing her titanic ass into the panties. The tiny thong string gorged into the flesh of her thick hips as it snuggled in between the folds of her mountainous ass cheeks.

"I'll be there around 7' o'clock to get you."

"Damn bitch! Why so early?" Miracle questioned, knowing the lounge wouldn't start jumping off until at least 9 o'clock. No females showed up early to a club to shake their asses, unless it was free for them until 12.

"Um..Excuse me! Because I know your greedy ass is gonna want to get something to eat before we get there." Heaven cited with confidence. Miracle couldn't say nothing, but laugh.

"Aw..You know a bitch so well." She admitted, making her way to the kitchen even as they spoke.

Miracle and Heaven had been best friends ever since childhood. They both grew up in the same foster home on the East Side of Wilmington, Delaware. It was there in an over crowed, two-bedroom, rat infested town house on Tenth and Pine Street, where their love and bond for each other grew stronger than sisters. And even though they were completely opposite in every way, their friendship was one of a kind and continued to blossom through-out the years. Heaven was the yin to Miracles yang, beautiful and petite with a honey-comb complexion and a backyard that could fit more than an outdoor pool. Heaven was the only person Miracle ever confided in about her insecurities about herself and Heaven always had encouraging words for her, no matter how low she sunk into the pits of her own degradation. Heaven always found a way to lift her back up.

"And speaking of food? Let me get off this phone so a I can feed my face, before a bitch's stomach start protesting like a Black Lives Matter rally. I'll holler at you later on bitch." Miracle said and hung up as she pillaged through the refrigerator looking for something fast and easy to cook..

She had settled on making a quick, but hefty breakfast of scrabbled eggs and bacon, along with a pot of grits smothered in butter and scarfed the meal down, just as fast as it touched her plate. *Damn! A bitch is still fucking hungry. I should of cooked the whole dozen of eggs.* She thought, rubbing her stomach as it rumbled with hunger pangs.

"Don't worry my love, mama gonna cook up something special for you tonight." She whispered, smiling down at her stomach. *Now your talking to your own stomach bitch? Yea you definitely need a nigga in your life.* She shook her head at her own thoughts and laughed as she washed the dirty dishes, then disappeared back upstairs into her bedroom. It wasn't long before she found herself spread across the bed, wide legged, with Mr. Long Stroke buried deep between her thighs as she fucked herself into an organic slumber.

Oh my God! What fucking time is it? Miracle thought, bolting upright in the bed and shooting a quick glance at the clock on the nightstand table. It read; Five-forty-five Pm. *Goddamn! What the hell I do, fuck myself into a coma?* Miracle jumped out of the bed and was about to rush off toward the bathroom to freshen up, Until the ringing of her phone stopped her dead in her tracks. *Fuck!* She thought, knowing it couldn't be nobody but Heaven calling to see if she was dressed and ready.

"What do you want bitch?" She answered with mock sarcasm as she hurriedly scrambled to get herself together.

"Bitch-h-h!-" Heaven replied, drawing out the word. "- I know your ass is not dressed and ready. I could hear you running around like a chicken with its head cut off." She accused and got laughter for a response as Miracle almost tripped over Mr. Long Stoke on the floor. She had totally forgotten about the dildo. She didn't even remember tossing it off the bed like discarded waste after she was done pleasuring herself.

"I am getting dressed now damn. Do you want to come see my naked ass getting dressed?" Miracle offered, picking up the wet stained dildo off the floor and chucking it back onto the bed.

"Ugh! That's a lil' too much ass for a bitch to be seeing." Heaven playfully joked, even though she had seen her best friend naked on many occasions. But tonight wasn't going to be one of those occasions. "Alright, I will be there in an hour to get you. And your ass better ready." She added and hung up without waiting for a reply. Miracle scoffed to herself. *A bitch can't rush perfection.* She thought, staring at the many designer fabrics inside of her closet. Her choices were complicated like a loveless romance. Shopping was her second biggest addiction, aside from food. She always had a misguided notion about her appearance, when it came to fashion. She once strongly believed, that designer clothes would make her look more appealing in the eyes of the opposite species, but later learned it wasn't the clothes that made a woman. It was a crushing blow of reality to her.

Miracle finally settled on a beautiful black Chanel dress to wear for the night. It was sleek and stylish with the perfect amount of flair, but it wasn't too flashy to draw a lot of attention to herself. Because attention was the last thing she wanted and tried her hardiest to shy away from in crowed places. Large gatherings held too many bad memories for her. Memories she would rather leave dead and forgotten. She dug up a pair of black pumps and set to work getting dressed, before Heaven shitted out a baby for her not being ready.

An hour later, she was pruned and prepped to go, but there was still no sign of Heaven. *An hour my ass!* She thought annoyed as she impatiently retraced her foot steps back to the window for the umpteeth time, and just as she was turning away, Heaven pulled into the driveway and sounded the horn. *About fucking time! A bitch is starving.* She thought as she rushed out of the front door and climbed into the front passenger seat of Heaven's X5-BMW.

"Bitch your late. I was about to cancel on your ass." She huffed in a tone sprinkled with attitude, forcefully closing the car door behind her. It slammed shut with a loud thud and rattled the car. Heaven threw her a dirty look.

"Bitch! You need to be worried about being late for your period. You and Mr. Long Stroke up in there." Heaven shot back to Miracle's surprise.

"Um..You know what?..I see you got jokes. Just drive bitch." Miracle was at lost for a witty come back and couldn't believe Heaven went there. *Real funny bitch!* She thought, returning her own dirty look and Heaven started laughing as she pulled into traffic and headed for the nearest eatery.

Of course, it was pass to ten O'clock when they finally arrived at the club Shades Of Blue, after their overly extended stay at Applebees, due to Miracles insatiable greedy ass and casually strolled inside of the club. The ever popular sound of old school reggae music greeted them as they entered.

"Oh my God! That's my shit!" Heaven shouted as the reggae artist Super Cat's voice chanted through the speakers. She started acting like a damn fool as she turned to face Miracle and begun gyrating against her body. Miracle was embarrassed. They haven't been inside the club for more than a second, before the ratchet side of Heaven suddenly appeared. And without notice.

Miracle hated dancing at clubs, because she never felt in-sync with the beat as though her jiggly form moved to a rhythm of its own. But she always found herself placed into that position, every time she went clubbing with Heaven. It was one of the reasons she constantly reneged on going out with her. She tried desperately hard to scatter away from the scene, but Heaven snatched her by the hand and pulled her back onto the dance floor.

"Damn! Can a bitch at least get a drink in her." Miracle whined at first, then loosened up as Heaven laughed and continued to dancing with her.

Five songs later, Miracle was tired and drenched in sweat. Her chubby feet was beyond the point of no return as her and Heaven made their way over to the bar and planted their asses onto a stool.

"Whew! You done wore a bitch out." Miracle breathed, wishing she had worn flats instead of pumps. She could no longer feel her pinkie toe and wondered if she left it on the dance floor. Heaven laughed. she was just getting the party started.

"Bitch! We turning up tonight!" Heaven exclaimed in a boisterous manner as they ordered their drinks and waited for them to arrive. Heaven could be over the top at times, even without the assistance of liquor in her system.

The club's atmosphere had a mellow, but yet, energetic vibe. It was pleasantly crowed, but not over bearably packed, and Miracle was thankful for that matter. Because the club Shades of Blue was notoriously known for violent out-breaks. She couldn't recount the many numbers of shootings that occurred there. It was like a saloon in the wild western days.

Heaven kept on constantly nudging her, pointing out, every fine looking man that swagged by the bar as they leisurely nursed on their drinks. To Miracle? Every last one of them was out of her league. So she never gave them a second glance. Heaven was always trying to be the match maker in her personal life, not that she cared, But it never seemed to worked and she struck out every time.

"Damn! I would love to take that nigga right there home with me tonight." Heaven drooled as she spied a tall dark and handsome nigga grooving alone on the dance floor. Miracle swiveled her head in the direction of the dance floor at the man in question. *Hmm..He look like he got some good tasty dick.* She thought to herself with a nasty intent. Heaven always had a knack for spotting easy prey. She was like a homing device when it cane to finding a piece of dick.

"I'll be right back bitch." Heaven hollered back over her shoulder as she made her way towards the dance floor.

Staring at her, Miracle shook her head in amusement and watched as Heaven rudely invaded the nigga's space with her ass pressed up against him. *This bitch is something else. Ratchet as hell. Always scheming on somebody's dick. But I love her to death.* She thought as she swallowed back her second glass of Sex On The Beach and was ready for another one. After ordering, she started growing bored watching everyone party on the dance floor and enjoying themselves, while she sat alone at the bar sharing a drink with loneliness. *I knew I should of kept my fat ass at home.* She thought, feeling neglected like an unwanted pregnancy. It was the untold story of her life.

"Excuse me beautiful, would you mind if I joined you?" A male voice asked, pulling her out of her lonely world and back into reality.

Miracle turned her gaze in the direction of the voice and looked into the face of a brown-skinned sexy man. At first, she thought he must be mistaken her for somebody else, until she realized he was staring directly at her with a smile on his face that could charm the pants off a nun. Immediately, her dark complexion turned a shade darker as she blushed and smiled back at him. She was stuck.

"Um..I don't see why not." She stammered shyly, as the feeling of boredom was far gone from her mind now. It was a whole new ball game.

"My name is Vincent, and yours beautiful lady?" He asked, extending out a hand. His sexy baritone voice caressed her large body like a spa bath. Making every nerve ending in her body tingle. *Oh my fucking God! His voice is so sexy.* Miracle thought she came inside of her panties.

"My name's Miracle and its nice to meet you." She replied in a small voice, tentatively shaking his out stretched hand. The softness of his hands touch sent her kitty spiraling out of control. But this time? There was no mistaken the wetness inside of her panties. Her lower floor region was long over due for a piece of wood.

Vincent was of average height, Mid-twenties, brown-skinned with a clean shaven head and intense brown eyes that shone bright with seduction. He had a muscular-athletic built tucked away under neath his form fitting shirt that was hard to conceal. And Miracle definitely took notice.

"The pleasure is all mine. Can I buy you another drink beautiful?" Vincent offered, casually occupying the stool Heaven recently vacated. *Beautiful? I know this nigga can't be talking about me? He must be blind and drunk, if he's calling me beautiful. Because a bitch haven't been called beautiful since a baby. And even then, it was said more out of politeness than a compliment.* Miracle thought as her insecure nature rose to the surface and she started feeling self-conscious about herself. To her? Every detail of her imperfections was visible in high-definition. Therefore, she was having a difficult time believing why a man as fine as Vincent would show the slightest interest in her. Less lone, call her beautiful?

"Yea, I wouldn't mind. I'll have a Sex On The Beach. Thank you." She gracefully accepted. Vincent flagged down the bartender and ordered both of them drinks.

"So, where are you from Miracle?" He asked, leaning in close to her so he could be heard over the loud music, as they both patiently waited on the bartender to deliver their drinks.

"I live on the North side. Jessup and Twenty-third street." She answered, hoping he couldn't hear the nervous tenor in her voice. *Relax bitch! it's just small-talk. Not a marriage proposal.* She told herself.

"Wow! Are you serious? I was born and raised on the North side. Twenty-eighth and Washington. I'm surprised I haven't seen you around the hood before?" He stated with a surprised expression on his face, as the bartender arrived and placed their drinks in front of them.

"I don't really hang outside that much. Besides going to work everyday, I spend most of my time in the house. There be too much bullshit happening outside for me. So I stay in my own lane." Miracle explained, reaching to take a sip of her drink. It was the forth one of the night.

"I definitely agree with you on that. It is too much shit going down on the north side of town. there has been a shooting every day this past week. It's crazy. But what got you out here tonight?" He asked, smiling at her with an intent gaze. The way he looked at her, made Miracle uncomfortable in her own skin. *Why is he looking at me like that? I hope I don't have a bugger in my nose.* She wondered with a false pretense of embarrassment. Miracle indiscreetly brushed a finger under her nose before she responded.

"I came here tonight with my best friend Heaven. She had been trying to get me to come to the club with her for awhile and I use to always tell her no, because I don't really do the club scene. It ain't for me. I am more of homebody than a party goer." She confided. Vincent's face melted into a playful expression.

"Or is because you don't know how to dance?" He teased, making her laugh.

"Boy bye! Don't let this bigness foul you. A bitch got a Beyonce in her step." She shot back laughing.

After awhile, Miracle started feeling buzzed and wasn't sure if it was from all the alcohol she consumed or from the way Vincent was making her feel inside. Either way, she was enjoying herself. It had been a long time since she enjoyed the company of a man.

"I like you Miracle and think you are a beautiful, intelligent woman and your funny as hell. You don't meet many woman like you, at least not now a days and I am happy that I met you tonight." He confessed, taking her hand into his and looked longingly into her eyes. Normally, Miracle would of taken offense to a stranger touching her, but his words had a profound impact on her as they verbally imprinted on her soul. A man had never spoken those kind of words to her before and she was at lost for words, speechless, until she found her voice.

"I really like you to Vincent and I am more happier than you that I met you." She admitted, meeting his gaze directly. A silent moment passed between them. But for Miracle? It was the moment the earth stood still and nothing else mattered as everything around her ceased to exist except for them.

There was no one, no music, no club, nothing. Just an emptiness quickly filling itself with him. Until, Heaven stumbled her way back over to the bar with a fresh catch in tow and shattered her illusory world.

"Damn! A bitch go to shake her tail feather and come back, and you got a whole fucking man!" Heaven declared to miracle, even though she was staring directly at Vincent as she spoke. Embarrassed, Miracle laughed shaking her head.

"Are you gonna introduce me to your new boo?" Heaven asked, standing with a hand propped on her curvy hip. Embarrassing Miracle even more. Vincent chuckled at her last comment.

"Vincent, this is my crazy ass best friend, Heaven. The one I was telling you about and Heaven, this is Vincent." Miracle introduced. "And I see your milkshake brought the boys to the yard." She added, slipping in her own jab.

"Oh! You ain't know? Every nigga want to go to heaven. And they ain't gotta die to get there!"" Heaven countered with a laugh. Immediately, Miracle knew heaven was totally wasted. Drunker than a sailor on a layover. She could hear it in her voice.

"Everybody this is Lance. Lance this is everybody." Heaven slurred. *Oh my God! She is so fucking disrespectful.* Miracle thought as her and Vincent looked at each other and started laughing. Heaven was a complicated piece of work.

The night had quickly danced away into the wee-hours of the morning and everybody was ready to called it a night as the crowd started thinning out. Heaven could barely stand up straight and had to lean on Miracle as they filed out of the club, but not before Miracle and Vincent exchanged phone numbers. The stray cat heaven adopted in the club, had a disappointed expression on his face as she abandoned him in the clubs parking lot and climbed into the car with Miracle. He looked crushed. There wasn't going to be any cat-nip for him tonight. It was a look Miracle grew well acquainted with; The face of rejection.

"I really had a good time tonight and enjoyed myself for the first time in awhile." Miracle beamed as she swung Heaven's X5 BMW out of the parking lot. Heaven was too drunk to drive, She could barely walk on her own, less lone steer a car and Miracle wasn't trying to be wrap around anybody's pole, unless it was Vincent's.

"Huh?..W-u-d-d-a   you   say?"   Heaven   slurred incoherently. She didn't hear a single word miracle had said.

Miracle swiveled her head and looked over at Heaven. She was slumped over sideways in the passenger seat with her head resting on the window's pane.

"Nothing drunk ass." Miracle said, pressing down hard on the gas peddle trying to beat the yellow traffic light. She was anxious to get home so she could shower and climb into bed. Her body was worn out like a stripper past her prime. Vincent had promised he would call her sometime tomorrow and she hoped he would, even though a part of her didn't expect him too. She was still having a hard time believing he really liked her and felt he only conversated with her out of pity, because there were a lot more prettier females at the club than her. What did he see in her that was so special? It was the million dollar question on her mind as she parked in front of her house and roused Heaven out of her drunken slumber.

Heaven had decided to spend the night at her house, because she was in no condition to drive all the way home, even though it was only a thirty minute drive. But to her? It might as well been a seven hour drive. As soon as they entered the house, Miracle kicked off her shoes, leaving them carelessly by the front door. Her poor chubby feet was killing her. Heaven managed to stumble her way onto the sofa and crashed, fully dressed. *Damn! The bitch ain't even take off her clothes.* Miracle thought, shaking her head as she made her way to the bedroom. *I'm surprised she even made it to the couch with her drunken ass.* She thought to herself as she wrestled out of her dress and crawled under the sheets in her lonely bed. The thought of showering was far from her mind as she pulled the silky sheets up around her shoulders. She was so tempted to scratch the persistent itch between her legs, but couldn't muster up the energy, because she was too exhausted. So instead, she stuffed a pillow in between her thighs and fell into a comfortable sleep.

CHAPTER TWO

It wasn't long before the sun peeked over the horizon, spilling a new morning as Miracle roused out of her sleep with a yawn and stretched. She stole a glance at the clock and it read: Eight-thirty Am. *Hell fucking no!* She thought, realizing she was only asleep for a couple of hours. She was about to duck back under the sheets and let sleep have its way with her for awhile, until she felt the wetness inside of her panties. *What the fuck?* She thought, reaching a hand down in-between her thighs to investigate. And sure as the sky was blue, her panties were soiled with cum. Shaking her head, she shimmed out of the bed and made a bee-line in the direction of the bathroom, thinking she must of had one hell of dream last night. Along the way she peeked in on Heaven, who was stretched across the couch fast asleep, snoring. Miracle was surprised, because she never figured her for the snoring type. *So pretty bitches do snore. I just hope her ass don't pee on my couch as well.* She laughed to herself as she headed into the bathroom and showered.

Heaven was fully alive and inside the kitchen cooking breakfast when she came back downstairs wearing nothing but a night gown, which left nothing to the imagination.

"Damn bitch! It took your ass longer than a month. What the fuck was you in there doing? Your nasty ass was probably in there making love to the shower?" Heaven accused teasingly as she walked into the kitchen.

"Its a long story." Miracle huffed. She was famished and whatever Heaven was cooking smelled delicious.

"You know a bitch love a good story."Heaven stated as she prepared both of them a plate. "And don't be stingy with the details."She added.

Miracle told her what she awoke to find inside the crotch of her panties and Heaven fell apart, almost dropping the plates of food on the kitchen floor. She couldn't stop herself from laughing.

"Oh! You think its real funny right bitch?" Even Miracle had to laugh at the embarrassing episode. *A wet fucking dream!* She mused.

"Bitch! You need some serious dick in your life. Some Vincent dick!" Heaven playfully teased as they both sat down at the table to eat. Miracle flicked Heaven the middle finger and started digging into the fish and grits Heaven cooked, but her thought wasn't on the food in front of her. The mentioning of Vincent's name, brought last night crashing back to the forefront of her mind.

"I don't want to rush things between me and Vincent. I really like him, but I don't think he's really into me and I don't want it to turn out like all my other failed relationships." Miracle expressed with a serious tone in her voice. Heaven shoved a bite of fish into her mouth before she spoke.

"Miracle, I really do think he's into you. I could tell by the way he was all over you last night and I think he would be good for you." Heaven explained. "Besides, your ass really do need some dick badly bitch!" She added with a goofy smirk on her face. Miracle almost choked on a folk full of grits as she laughed.

"Fuck you too Heaven!" She shot back through a spurt of coughs, spraying half chewed food particles of across the table.

"Ugh! Damn bitch!" Heaven complained with disgust as she examined her food looking for whatever flew out of Miracle's mouth, because she wasn't trying to accidentally swallow nothing toxic.

"Suck on that bitch!" Miracle laughed and continued scrapping at her plate as though nothing ever happened.

After they were done eating and bullshitting, Heaven washed the dishes, then got ready to go home so she could shower and get dressed.

"I will call you later. Love you girl." Heaven said as she headed out of the front door.

"Alright. Love you back." Miracle replied, locking the door behind her. Miracle shuffled into the living room and sat on the sofa, bored. She thought about reading the new Urban Novel, "Twisted Treasures" By the Author JC Pipkin, that she had recently purchased on line, but decided against it. Instead, she turned on the 70 inch flat screen television and surfed through the channels, until she landed on the reality show Hip-Hop Atlanta. *Oh yea! These mother fuckers are crazy.* She thought, watching the heated argument unfolding on the screen. *Karlie red is a hot mess.* She laughed, getting comfortable on the sofa and settled into the show.

Miracle couldn't remember the last time she watched the show and decided to catch up on the episodes she had missed, until her phone rang interrupting her Atlanta moment. *What the hell Heaven want now? She just fucking left!* She fumed, tempted to ignore the call and let it go to voice mail. *I swear she's a hot damn mess!* She thought, picking up the phone.

"Damn bitch! You just walked out the door. Its nowhere near later." She barked as soon as she answered.

"Um..Excuse me? May I speak to Miracle please?" A male voice asked. Embarrassed, Miracle quickly looked at the caller Id and immediately recognized the number. It was Vincent. *Oh Shit!* She thought and placed the phone back to her face.

"Oh my God! I'm so sorry Vincent. I thought you was Heaven's crazy ass." She apologized with an embarrassing giggle, even though inside she was jumping up and down. She was surprised that he called, and so soon. *There might be a chance after all.* She thought with a childish grin on her face.

"Its okay beautiful. I hope I didn't catch you at a bad time. But I couldn't get you out off my mind and decided to call you so I could hear your voice." He confessed. Hearing his words, her heart skipped faster than a scratched record as butterflies flapped in the grassy field of her stomach. It was like his words verbally imprinted on her soul.

"No you didn't catch me at a bad time. I am actually happy you called, because I couldn't stop thinking about you either." She breathed, feeling like she was hyperventilating. *A bitch even had a wet dream about you.* She wanted to add, but kept it to herself. She didn't want to seem too desperate for some of his dick. At least not yet.

"I also called to see if you wanted to go out to dinner with me tonight?" He asked. *Dinner? Hell yea I would love to go to dinner! A bitch love to eat.* She thought more excited than the little fat boy from the movie; "Charlie and The Chocolate Factor." she felt like she won the golden ticket.

"Yes. I would love too. What time?" She agreed, smiling so hard her chubby cheeks started hurting. *I'm going out...I'm going out!* She sang inside of her head as she responded to him, and hope he couldn't hear the eagerness in her voice.

"How do eight o'clock sound?" He said.

"That will be fine." She confirmed, feeling as though her body was floating through the ceiling. She was elated.

Eventually, after an hour on the phone talking about everything and nothing, they finally said their goodbyes and hung up. Even though Miracle felt like she could've stayed on the phone with him forever. She couldn't wait to share the latest news with Heaven as she happily pranced around the living room, looking like an oversize ballerina. She was still chanting the melody inside of her head. The reality show on TV was now watching her acting like a damn fool as she danced her way upstairs into the bedroom. She started shopping early inside of her closet for the perfect outfit to wear for the night, when her phone suddenly rang again. The sound of the ringing caused a forlorn feeling to rise in the pit of her stomach. *I knew the shit was to fucking good to be true.* She thought, assuming it was Vincent calling right back to cancel their dinner date. But it wasn't. It was Heaven. Miracle breathed a sigh of relief as she answered the phone.

"Hey what's up girl?"

"Shit, my bad for not caller sooner. But a bitch just woke back up." Heaven explained.

"Its all good. Guess what bitch? Vincent called me a little while ago and asked me to go to dinner with him tonight." Miracle exclaimed with excitement.

"Get the fuck out of here! I am so happy for you. I told you the nigga was feeling you, and bitch, you better get some dick for dessert. Because God knows you need it. Especially after this mornings episode." Heaven cracked in a joking manner.

"Bitch! You got too much dick on your mind." Miracle retorted with a laugh, then fell quite as she heard a gruff male voice in the background of the line.

"Bitch who is that? You was sleeping my ass!" She accused and Heaven started laughing.

"Bye bitch!" Heaven fired back quickly and hung up, disconnecting the line. *She's a nasty bitch!* Miracle thought shaking her head as she continued dumpster diving inside of her closet.

CHAPTER THREE

Miracle couldn't believe how fast the evening had rolled around. Eight O'clock came faster than she expected. She was a bundle of nervous energy as she paced the living room floor waiting on Vincent to arrive. A part of her believed he wasn't coming and was almost convinced of it, until she heard the knock at the front door. *Oh my God! He really came.* She thought, trying to steady the pounding of her heart as she hurried and opened the door.

"Hey beautiful." Vincent crooned, standing in the threshold of the doorway holding a bouquet of roses. Stunned, Miracle was lost for words. No man had ever brought her flowers before in her life.

"Oh my God! They are so beautiful Vincent. Thank you." She beamed, accepting the roses with tears pooling in her eyes. Miracle had always been sensitive as a fragile snowflake. She rushed into his arms and he held her tightly.

"Always beautiful." He said, embracing her close.

After what seemed like an eternity in his arms, she regrettably broke the embrace, even though she was reluctant to do so, because she wanted to stay in his arms forever. But it wasn't something her stomach was about to permit. She was starving. She took the flowers inside the house and placed them on the kitchen counter, then followed closely behind Vincent as they walked back outside to his car. Immediately, she was impressed by the type of vehicle he drove. It was an old school black Chevy Capri with 22 inch chrome rims.

Vincent disabled the alarm and held open the front passenger side door for her. Miracle was taken aback by the gesture. It was the first time a man held a car door open for her and it made her feel special. *Damn! This nigga got a bitch falling in love with him already.* She thought.

"Thank you." She gushed as she climbed into the car.

"My pleasure beautiful." Vincent quipped closing the door and jogged around to the other side. Miracle couldn't stop herself from blushing every time he called her beautiful. It was something she had to get use too.

"So where are we going?" She asked Vincent as he pulled into traffic.

"Its a nice little restaurant called; Eclipse Bistro. Trust me, you are gonna love the food there." He assured. Eclipse Bistro's was one of the oldest and best Italian restaurant in Delaware. It was tucked away in the quiet suburbs of Newark, Delaware.

Vincent parked in front of the restaurant and climbed out of the car. Walking around, he opened the door for Miracle and took her hand as they casually walked inside the establishment. Miracle felt so special. It was the first time a man held her hand in public. She couldn't keep herself from smiling like a bubbly infant. They had found a vacant table tucked away in the far corner of the restaurant and occupied it. The savory aroma's in the air had Miracle's stomach doing somersaults. She couldn't wait to taste the delicious smelling food.

The waiter had brought over menu's and they browsed through it, until they both settled on a meal of fish and pasta. It was rumored to be the restaurants signature dish. After placing their orders, they indulged themselves in light conversation until their food had arrived. The fish and pasta smelled ravishing, and Miracle was ready to chow down as her eyes feasted on the tasty looking dish. She wasted no time digging into her meal and found it to be delicious as it was rumored to be.

"Hmm..This is really good!" She chirped, scooping another folk full into her mouth. Vincent chuckled. He was happy she enjoyed it.

After many bites and swallows later, Miracle took a sip of the red wine and looked intensely at Vincent. She had a far away look in her eyes and it caught his attention.

"Are you okay beautiful?" He asked with a timber concern in his voice.

"Huh?..Oh, I am fine. I was just thinking that's all." She assured him. But he could tell there was something weighing heavy on her mind.

"Miracle, you do know that you could talk to me right?.. About anything." He expressed. There was sincerity in his voice. Miracle fell quiet for a long moment, before she spoke.

"I still can't believe that a fine looking man like you is interested in me. And the night at the club when you first spoke to me? I thought you was talking to someone else, especially when you called me beautiful-" Miracle paused and took a deep breath before she continued. "-It all feels so unreal. Like I am dreaming and I am going to wake up to find you are only in my imagination and it makes me so scared." She confided, trying to swallow down the lump in her throat. But the tears in her voice was as visible as if they were running down her face.

Vincent was moved by the honesty of her words as he leaned back and looked deep into her eyes. And for the first time, he noticed the sorrow and loneliness inside of them. He couldn't image all she had been through in her life.

"Miracle, listen to me. I truly think you are a beautiful woman and I mean this with all my heart. I am a grown man and know exactly what I want and who I want. And that person is you Miracle. So you don't have to wonder no more if its a dream, because I am as real as the air you breathe and so is the feelings I have for you and the relationship I want share with you." He expressed, taking hold of her hand from across the table. His words broke her. She couldn't hold back the tears any longer as they spilled over the rims of her eyes and ran freely down her cheeks. They were the tears of the most happiest moment of her life. And to her, nothing else in the world mattered. She was deeply in love with Vincent.

Later that night, Vincent drove Miracle back home and walked her to the front door of her house.

"I really do hope you enjoyed yourself tonight. Because I definitely enjoyed spending time with you. And I look forward to us doing it again real soon." He suggested planting a gentle kiss on her forehead and turning to walk away.

"Vincent!-" She called after him. He stopped and turned around to face her. "-I would love it if you stayed the night with me." She offered in a small and meek voice, knowing how much she desperately wanted his comforting presence.

"I would love too." He accepted and followed her into the house.

Once inside, She gave Vincent a brief tour of her humble home. It was spacious and beautifully furnished. Vincent was impressed by the taste of her décor as she showed him around, room by room. Afterwards, she led him upstairs where they both retired in the bedroom. But not before she placed the bouquet of roses he gave her into a vase with water.

"I'll give it to you Miracle, you have a beautiful home." He complimented as he stood before her and slowly peeled out of his clothes. *Oh my fucking God! He got a sexy ass body!* She thought and immediately started feeling self-conscious about the way her own body looked, and was hesitant to get undressed in front of him. It had been ages since a man seen her naked. But to Vincent, he thought she was uncomfortable with the idea of them sleeping with each other on the first night.

"Miracle listen, we don't have to have sex understand? I don't want us to rush into anything too fast. I would be satisfied with just cuddling with you. So you don't have to be uncomfortable with me." He addressed, smiling at her reassuringly. *Cuddling? I want you to fuck a bitch so good, it would leave me permanently crippled!* Her carnal mind thought, but she was too shy and afraid to say it to him aloud. Even though the stirring between her legs was throbbing to another tune. She quickly undressed and slithered into bed beside him, ignoring the sexual urges as she snuggled closely against him.

Early the next morning, Miracle awoke to a full service of breakfast in bed. Except, she was the dish being served as Vincent's tongue tickled and teased her sensitive clit. At first, Miracle thought she was having another one of her wet dreams, but the feeling of pleasure felt too real. Her body shook, involuntarily, and she moaned into the reality of his tongue as it tenderly flicked in circular motions across the surface of her woman hood. *Oh..Oh God!* Her thoughts screamed and she became fully aware of every sensation as it coursed through the forgotten region between her legs. The feeling of pleasure was over powering as her back arched high off the mattress, and her thick thighs trembled under the seducing assault of his tongue. *What is he doing to me?..Oh God!* She cried inside, clutching tightly at the sheets as his mouth work a Miracle On 34th Street.

"Oh!.. fuck daddy!..Eat this pussy." She panted, writhing as though her soul was in agony from the fiery pleasure of his tongue. She could feel the mounting waters of an orgasm as it rose deep inside of her loins. Growing and growing, until it burst, sending her over the edge of its waterfall into the river below.

"Ooh!..Ooh!..Ooh!" Miracle howled like a wolf under a full moon as she washed away in the tide of an orgasm. She couldn't stop her body from shaking.

Vincent arose from between her legs with his mouth glistening in a frothy wetness and climbed in-between her trembling legs. He took hold of her massive thighs, spreading them farther apart and entered deep inside of her most sacred place.

"Ooh!.. Shit!" Her face morphed into a masked grimace of pain as he plunged his huge shaft deep inside of her hole. The subtle pain had awakened the sleeping pleasure that lied dormant inside of her forsaken cunt, as the thickness of him stretched opened her virgin tight hole. The pain felt so unbearably good. She wrapped her arms around his slim chiseled waist and held him tight as he made love to her soul. Miracle broke like a fragile vase as he steadily stroked deep inside of her, while kissing her with such a ferocious passion, that she swore her spirit was rising out of her body. Tears of pure ecstasy ran freely unchecked down her chocolate coated face. Inside of her, it felt as though a poetry of words were being permanently etched on her soul.

"Oh God!" Miracle cried out, digging her manicured nails into the flesh of Vincent's back as his steady thrusting became rapid like over worked pistons in overdrive. She started bucking wildly beneath him, meeting each of his thrust with her own, as he relentlessly pounded hard inside of her.

She could feel the angry throbbing of his manliness swell inside of her and knew he was ready to unleash his pent up load. So she lifted and spread her legs farther apart, giving him full access to her chocolate kitty.

"I want to feel your cum deep inside of me." Miracle purred, clawing at the silk sheets like a black-footed wild cat as he pumped harder and faster inside of her.

"Oh yes!..Fuck me daddy!" Miracle spurred him on as she felt the pressure from him pounding deep inside of her stomach. The pressure was surmounting as it engulfed her in a cocoon of pleasure and she shuddered, as a powerful orgasm quaked through out her entire body, causing her to squirt like a tsunami crashing violently against the shore.

"Ooh!..Shit!..Ooh Fuck!" She moaned, soaking the entire lower half of the mattress as Vincent grunted and shot his seed close behind her. Afterwards, they both laid spent in each others arms cuddling.

Miracle had never felt more safe in the embrace of a mans arms and didn't want him to ever let go of her. She felt like she could rest in his arms forever. Hours had slowly drifted into the afternoon as they laid quietly snuggled up against one another, until the annoying ringing of her phone disturbed the tranquil silence. *Damn! Who the fuck is blowing my phone up?* She thought agitated. She was tempted not to answer it, because she didn't want to move out of Vincent's arms. But the persistent ringing was disrupting her serene moment. So she reached over his prone body and snatched the phone off the nightstand table and answered it.

"Hello?"

"Damn bitch! I was about to hang up. What are you doing?" It was Heaven.

"Nothing. Right now I am just laying down relaxing. Why? Whats up" Miracle asked with a curious tone.

"Laying down? Bitch you need to get your ass up and come with me to the mall. I saw these nice ass shoes I want to get and.." Heaven abruptly paused as she heard a muffled cough in Miracle's background. At first, She thought she was tripping and looked at the phone in her hand as if it suddenly sprouted two heads. "-Bitch! Who the fuck are you laid up with Huh? And don't lie because I heard someone in the background." Heaven said matter of factly.

"Stop being nosy bitch! You tripping. You ain't hear shit!? It was probably some other strange nigga your laying up with." Miracle denied with a defensive tone, even though she was burning to tell her. It was flaming on the tip of her tongue, until it got too hot for her hold any longer.

"Its Vincent." She finally confessed with a beaming smile in her voice.

"Bitch! No the fuck you didn't. Let me find out!" Heaven screamed in shock on the other end of the phone. "So I see you got that dessert dick after all." She teased with laughter.

"Whatever bitch! Bye!" Miracle shot back and hung up laughing. She crawled back into the arms of Vincent and he held her closely, staring into her beautiful eyes with a mischievous smile on his face.

"What?" She asked blushing and got an immediate response, when he quietly leaned in closer and kissed her on the lips...Longingly, filling her with want.

CHAPTER FOUR

A month had quickly flew pass since Miracle and Vincent became a permanent fixture together. They were inseparable. It was impossible to see one of them without seeing the other, and their love for each other blossomed into a beautiful relationship. But for Miracle? Everyday seemed surreal. It felt like she was living the real life of Cinderella and Vincent was her Prince Charming. It was a fairy tale feeling and she wanted to pinch herself everyday to make sure she wasn't dreaming, because it was a feeling she was afraid of losing. she was so much happier in her life now and couldn't remember the last time she ever felt that way.

There was a glow of happiness to her and she radiated with a self-love that slowly chiseled away at her self-consciousness. It was like she was fully awake for the first time in her life and seeing her true beauty, inside and out. Because she had found a man that loved her despite all of her imperfections.

Miracle strutted into the bathroom with a colorful spring in her step and Slipped out of her pink terry cloth robe. And stared at herself in the bathroom mirror and barely recognized the woman staring back at her. A month ago she would of cringed at her reflection and felt disgusted with herself as her insecurities would of stood mockingly glaring back her. But those days was long past as she stared at the beauty of her dark chocolate complexion. It was like seeing herself for the first. She no longer seen the imperfections that teased every inch of her body and saw the craftsmanship of God's hand in her curvy plumpness. She smiled to herself as she climbed into the bubble bath and soaked in her happiness. But it wasn't long before the ringing of her phone interrupted her, me-time, moment. *Oh my God!* She sighed as she reached and answered the call.

"Hello?"

"Damn! That's all a bitch get is a constipated hello?" It was Heaven. Miracle laughed as she listened to her whine. She haven't seen Heaven in weeks since her and Vincent became like Siamese cats.

"I didn't sleep with your ass last night and I damn sure didn't eat your pussy!" Heaven joked feigning an attitude.

"Girl bye! You know damn well you want this chocolate eclair." Miracle shot back with laughter.

"I haven't seen you in awhile Miracle and I'm starting to feel neglected. You done got some good dick in your life and now you acting all bougie and shit. I miss my bestie." Heaven complained.

"Bitch, you know ain't nothing change but my soaked stained panties. I miss you too and I'm sorry I haven't been a friend lately or had a moment to chill with you. But a bitch been busy and caught up with that nigga Vincent." Miracle explained as she smiled knowingly to herself, replaying the nasty episodes of her life's first season of love in her mind. Heaven sucked her teeth through the phone.

"Let me find out your jealous." Miracle teased.

"Jealous? Please! You know a bitch got niggas stuck on this clit like fleas on a dog." Heaven slung back and Miracle broke broke down in laughter. She was definitely speaking the truth.

Heaven was a certified bad bitch and ever since childhood niggas been chasing after her like she was the American dream. So growing up, Miracle felt like she was the beast in their friendship, but Heaven always found a way to make her feel wanted and loved.

"But for real bitch when am I gonna see you?" Heaven asked with a seriousness in her tone.

"We don't got nothing planned for this weekend, so we can definitely hang out then."

"We? When the fuck did you turn french bitch? I was talking about us, me and you. Not your new found dick." Heaven blasted sarcastically.

"Fuck you heifer! Is that french enough for you bitch? I will see your crazy ass tomorrow, because tonight Vincent's taking me to meet his mother."

"His mother?" Heaven hissed and Miracle could tell she had her face scrunched up in her usual fashion as she spoke.

"Let me find out the nigga is trying to wife you up." She quipped and started singing the song; **Be my wifey** by the R&B singer Next. *Oh this bitch really got jokes!* Miracle thought laughing as heaven sang off key.

"Bye bitch! My water is getting cold." Miracle scoffed and hung up to heaven's laughter.

Miracle climbed out of the cold tub water after washing and toweled off, then strutted naked into her bedroom with a purpose. She fished through her drawer and snagged a cute Veronica Ann panties set and wiggled into them. She was undecided as to what outfit to wear as she gazed at the wardrobe of designer fabrics inside of her closet. She didn't want to come across too flashy or sluttish when she met Vincent's mother, because first impressions was lasting ones. She wanted his mother to like her for who she was and not for what she was wearing. *That'll be perfect!* She thought as she settled on a sleek, but elegant black Louis Vuitton blouse and a pair of black denim jeans. She knew the color black was an illusory color on big woman and made them look slimmer, so it was definitely the right color of choice.

After She was done getting dressed, She admired her handy work in the mirror and smiled to herself. *A bitch looking fat- fabulous!* She thought loving the woman staring back at her.

"Hey beautiful." She gushed aloud blowing her reflection a kiss. Miracle was really feeling herself. *Damn! I'm starving!* She thought as she followed her stomach into the kitchen and had an affair with last nights left-over roast and macaroni cheese. It was the only time she cheated on the love of her life. Food was the one exception to the rule.

As she lifted the fork and was about to swallow back the last mouthful food on the plate, her phone rang. Irritated, She reached for the phone. Miracle didn't to be disturbed when she was eating. It was like someone busting into the room in the middle of an orgasm.

"Hello?" She answered, trying to keep the edge out off her voice as her stomach cussed and complained.

"Hows my beautiful baby doing?" Vincent crooned sexily. Miracle's attitude had quickly melted like ice in the summer sun as soon as she heard his voice.

"I'm fine. But I would be even better once I'm snuggled in your arms." She breathed feeling the stirring tempest building deep inside of her. *Oh God! What has he done to me?* She thought as Vincent laughed.

"Don't worry beautiful, we have all night to play. Are you dressed and ready? My mother is dying to meet you."

"Yea baby I'm dressed and ready. Just waiting on you to get here."

"Okay cool. I will be there in a little while to pick you up. But I have to make quick stop first along the way and make sure you have room to eat because my mother is cooking a small feast." He said with a laugh. Vincent's mother loved to cook. *A bitch always got room to eat!* Miracle thought as she finished off her plate.

"Don't worry I will be bringing along my appetite as well." She promised and hung up feeling giddy inside. Miracle happily shuffled around the kitchen cleaning up as she waited on Vincent to arrive.

Vincent's mother lived in a nice modest home in the suburbs of Bear, Delaware. It was peaceful and quiet. A refreshing change from the crime infested area of the city of Wilmington, where the streets were riddled with bullets and junkies. As Vincent pulled into the driveway and parked, Miracle admired the two-story stucco home and lavish landscape. It was definitely a visual vacation from the North side of Wilmington. Vincent escorted Miracle onto the front porch where his mother stood waiting in the doorway with a smile on her face as bright as the sunshine.

"Hey baby how are you? I knew I heard somebody pull into the driveway." His mother beamed happily, giving him an affectionate hug before pulling away and gazing longingly at Miracle.

The way she looked at Miracle made her feel self-conscious and she didn't know whether to smile or run back to the car. But, before she could make up her mind his mother spoke.

"So this must be the lovely Miracle your constantly telling me about?" She addressed to Vincent, while still gazing fondly at Miracle. *Constantly telling her about? Damn! This nigga must really do love me.* Miracle thought as Vincent's mothers words washed away the feeling of her self-consciousness.

"Yea ma' this is my beautiful Miracle and Miracle this is my mother Elaine." He introduced as his mother led them into the house.

"Hi, its nice to meet you Mrs. Elaine." Miracle said coyly with downcast eyes.

"Girl, Call me anything but Mrs! You make me feel old and I'm far from old, I could still can down with the best of them. I maybe Firty-two, but I can still snag a young roaster." Mrs. Elaine chided with a hand on her thick hip. Miracle couldn't stop herself from laughing as Vincent shook his head in embarrassment at his mothers antics.

"But its nice to finally meet you too sweat heart. And boy, you better take that look off your face. How the hell you think you got here." Mrs. Elaine playfully scolded Vincent as they followed behind her into the kitchen.

Miracle had instantly took a liking to his mother and thought she was funny and crazy as hell. She reminded her of a foster aunt, Caroline. Caroline was a piece of work, but Miracle loved her and missed her from time to time. But what sealed the deal for her stomach was the delicious aroma of pepper steak and rice brewing on the stove. *Greedy ass bitch!* She chastised herself as she planted her thickness into a chair at the table. Vincent found a vacant seat across from her as his mother prepared their plates. Miracle felt like she was a million miles apart from him, instead of right across the table as she stared at him. But to her, it might as well been the Atlantic Ocean that separated them. *Relax bitch! He ain't going nowhere.* She told herself.

"Are you okay beautiful?" Vincent asked with a trace of concern in his voice. He hoped his mothers craziness didn't make her feel uncomfortable.

"Huh?..Oh I'm good baby." She blushed, feeling like a Peeping Tom getting caught staring into a window.

Vincent gave her quizzical look. He knew there was something on her mind, because of the expression on her face.

"What?" She asked hesitantly, wondering why he was looking at her questioningly. But before he could respond his mother placed their plates onto the table.

"I hope you like spicy food Miracle, because this here child goes in hot and comes out even hotter. If you know what I mean." Mrs. Elaine warned with a playful seriousness. *Shit! ain't nothing hotter than whats stirring between a bitch's legs.* Miracle thought as she laughed and stared at Vincent with nasty intentions.

"I love spicy foods Mrs. Elaine." Miracle admitted, taring her eyes away from Vincent. Mrs. Elaine placed a delicate hand over her heart and stared at Miracle with a feigned expression of hurt on her face.

"Girl! What did I tell you about calling me Mrs.?" She scolded taking a seat at the head of the table.

"I'm sorry Mrs..Um..Mama Elaine." Miracle stammered feeling admonished like a child.

"Boy you hear that? I done got myself a daughter-n-law." Mrs. Elaine bragged to Vincent's embarrassment. *A daughter-n-law?* Miracle thought as Heaven's words replayed in her mind and her heart started fluttering like a field of butterflies. *I know this niggas not gonna propose to me?* She wondered doubtfully, even though every fiber of her soul wanted him too.

"Ma' don't start." Vincent quickly retorted shaking his head. Mrs. Elaine laughed heartily. She was always trying to marry him off to someone and wished he would find a decent woman to settle down with and have kids. Because she desperately wanted grand babies. But Vincent suffered from the same genetic defect as his father did; A whoring gene. *Poor girl.* Mrs. Elaine thought as she dug into her plate along with everyone else.

The kitchen was bathed in silence, besides the scrapping sounds of forks against plates as everyone ate quietly in their own thoughts. Miracle couldn't stop stealing fugitive glances at Vincent as she ate, and it didn't go unnoticed by Mrs. Elaine. She could tell Miracle was head over heels in love with her son, because it poured out of her pours stronger than the stench of an alcoholic in the morning. *I pray that boy don't hurt this poor girl.* Mrs. Elaine prayed before she cleared her throat and spoke.

"So Miracle how do you like the food?" Mrs. Elaine asked innocently as Vincent excused himself from the table and ascended the stairs towards the bathroom.

"The food taste really good Mama Elaine. I love it." Miracle admitted as she shoved another forkful into her mouth.

"I know your mothers cooking must be just as good." Mrs. Elaine commented. Miracle fell quiet for a brief moment and Mrs. Elaine hoped she didn't offend her by prying.

"Um..My mother passed away giving birth to me, So I never got the chance to know or even meet her." Miracle finally said with a note a sadness in her voice.

"Oh my God! I am truly sorry to hear that child. My condolences." Mrs. Elaine gasped, feeling remorseful for bringing up the subject. She couldn't image the hardship Miracle must of went through growing up without a mother.

"Its alright Mama Elaine. I've learned to live with it." Miracle expressed. But Mrs. Elaine knew better. No child could truly live without a mothers nutrient love. *Dear lord, this poor girl.* Mrs. Elaine's heart went out to her.

"How is Vincent treating you?" Mrs. Elaine inquired, taking the opportunity to have a heart to heart talk with her while Vincent was out of ear shot.

The question caught Miracle off guard as she heard the seriousness in Mrs. Elaine's tone and felt cornered like a helpless mouse being interrogated by hungry cat.

"And you can be honest with me baby, because I know that boy can be a handful." She added, trying to sooth the worried expression Miracles face. *Oh my God! I can't believe she's asking me this.* Miracle thought as she tried to gather the right words to say.

"Um..To be perfectly honest with you Mama Elaine, Vincent is the best man I ever been in a relationship with. The way he treats me and even looks at me make me feel more special than anyone ever made me feel in my life-" Miracle started choking up and had to pause to gather herself together because her emotions started running on high, before she continued. "-I never thought I would find a man like him Mama Elaine. Someone that loves me for me, despite the imperfection I have. I know I don't look like those model types, but he makes me feel like I do and that in itself means the world to me." Miracle conveyed, batting away a lone tear that crept down her cheek.

Good God, Thank you Jesus! Mrs. Elaine thought as she sat there speechless. She was lost for words. She couldn't believe what she heard about her son. It was as though a new morning arose without her, and she wondered if her son was finally coming to his senses. Mrs. Elaine rose from the table and hugged Miracle tight, rocking her gently in her arms as Miracle sobbed on her shoulders. Mrs. Elaine knew she cried the tears of happiness.

"Child, when you find that special love with the right person in this world, you hold onto it with dear life. Because the devil will do anything to steal away the precious gift God has blessed you with. You hear me? You fight hard until you can't fight no more and then you fight even harder." Mrs. Elaine whispered encouragingly as a mother into her ear as she held her. Miracle only nodded, because she didn't trust her voice to speak as she stood there sobbing on Mrs. Elaine's caring shoulder.

A long moment had passed before they broke their embrace, but not before a mother and daughter bond was silently forged between them. As they went about gathering the finished plates off the table, Miracles phone chirped inside of her pocket and she excused herself as she peeked at the notification. It was from Vincent. *Why is he texting me?* She wondered as she opened and read the text message:

"Meet me in the bathroom!"

Miracle gasped. She couldn't believe what he texted and read the message a second time before she caught the meaning of his intent. *Oh my fucking God! I know this nigga ain't talking about what I think he is?* She mused and immediately felt the embers between her legs ignite and spread through-out her body like a wild brush fire. She looked at Mrs. Elaine and noticed that she was watching her with a worried expression on her face.

"Is everything alright baby?" Mrs. Elaine asked concerned. *Everything is perfect. But would you mind if I fucked your son in the bathroom?* Miracle wanted to say, but kept her sinful thoughts to herself.

"Yes everything is fine Mama Elaine. Do you mind if I use the bathroom?"

"Go right on ahead. I'll finish up the rest of these dishes." Mrs. Elaine assured her with a smile playing at the corners of her mouth. Miracle hesitated. There was something in the way Mrs. Elaine said it that kept her rooted in place. *Do she know?* Miracle wondered as she looked at the tell-tale smile playing on her face and was about to text Vincent back and say no...Until her phone chirped again.

Miracle already knew who it was from and gave in, as the throb between her legs grew more persistent. Eagerly, She made her way upstairs and headed towards the bathroom. There was an urgency in her stride, as though every step was in sync with the pulse throbbing between her thick thighs. As she approached the bathroom door it swung open and Vincent stood there with a mischievous smile on his face and miracles heart started pounding loudly in her chest, but not as loud as the thumping between her legs. It was a nervous excitement.

"What took you so long? I started to think you stood a nigga up." He presumed as Miracle slid past him into the bathroom.

"I never been the type of bitch to pass up some good dick." She boasted with false confidence as she tried to swallow down a large cup of jitters. Vincent laughed as he closed and locked the door behind them.

Miracle was surprised to find the bathroom so spacious and was thankful, because being a big bitch and trying to sneak a quickie in a small ass bathroom wasn't about to work. Especially not with her Seventy inch ass.

"What about your mother?" She asked with a jumpy pitch in her voice as she looked around the bathroom with nervous suspicion. *Calm down bitch, she ain't watching y'all.* She scolded herself.

"What about her?"

"She's right downstairs and the-" Vincent silenced her with a kiss, burying his tongue deep into her mouth as he pushed her up against the wall, while his hands expertly roamed her body. Miracle was too weak to protest as her body succumbed to his caressing touch. She started feeling faint as the stirring inside of her swelled, becoming over powering as she lost her resolve to resist. *Oh God!* She shuddered.

Miracle fumbled with the constraints on her pants, fighting to wiggle them down around her thick thighs as Vincent led her towards the bathtub. She bent over planting her hands on the rim of the tub, exposing the fullness of her round chocolate buns as he positioned himself behind her and guided his dick deep into her welcoming hole.

"Oh fuck!" Miracle moaned as his thick wood splintered her tight pussy, stretching open the small orifice as he recklessly and mercilessly pounded inside her.

"Goddamn daddy!" She cried out gripping the rim of the tub with her pudgy hands as he slammed roughly inside of her causing her legs to tremble with each hard thrust. She could feel the mounting pressure in her stomach as his dick banged against her cervix, leaving her lost in a state of wild ecstasy.

Vincent gripped her wide spread hips and repeatedly slammed ten-inches of angry dick deep inside of her causing her knees to buckle as he beat her womanhood like an abusive husband.

"Ooh, shit!.. Yes, daddy!.. Fuck this pussy!" Miracle screeched as the sound of smacking flesh echoed off the bathroom walls like a thick leather belt whipping against a naked back. She could feel the on rushing orgasm speeding towards her like a roaring train as she quivered and tried to brace herself for the head on collision. *Ooh fuck! I can't take it no more!* She thought as the fiery pleasure coursed through her with the intensity of a burning furnace.

"Ooh!..Ooh!..Ooh! Fuck daddy!" She moaned loudly, forgetting her surroundings as her guttural shriek vibrated through-out the bathroom and she collapsed into the tub as the powerful aftermath of the orgasm buckled her knees underneath of her.

"Shit!" She cussed plummeting forward as Vincent tumbled closely behind her into the tub. It was a comical moment and they both started laughing as they tried to pick themselves up. It was an awkward looking situation and Miracle felt slightly embarrassed with her whole wheat buns hiked high in the air. She couldn't believe what happened.

"Are you okay?" Vincent asked with amusement in his voice. He was trying hard not laugh at how Miracle looked as he helped her out of the tub and he was thankful she cushioned his fall.

"Yea I'm alright." She assured him, accepting his help as he pulled her up. *Now a bitch know how a beached whale feels.* She thought shaking her head in humiliation as she straightened out her disheveled appearance.

"Do you think your mother heard us?" She asked with a worried look on her on face, because that was the last thing she needed right now, for his mother to know she was fucking her son in the bathroom and damn near broke the tub in the process.

"Nah, I don't think she heard anything. And besides, it wasn't that loud." He asserted, but Miracle wasn't convinced. *Think? What the fuck do he mean think?*

She thought as they exited the bathroom and went back downstairs.

As Miracle walked into the kitchen with Vincent close at her heels, she tried to act innocent as if nothing happened in the bathroom as she quietly sat back at the table. Mrs. Elaine turned in Miracles direction and looked at her with a knowing smile on her beautifully aged face. The glint inside of her hazel colored eyes spoke its meaning without words.

"Is everything alright baby?-" Mrs. Elaine asked Miracle, then turned to Vincent as he busied himself looking into the refrigerator. "-Boy get narrow behind out my refrigerator and what the hell was that loud noise upstairs?" She inquired. *Oh my fucking God! she heard us.* Miracle thought humiliated.

"Um...Yea-I mean yes everything is okay Mama Elaine." The words staggered clumsily out of her mouth like a drunk as Vincent waved his mother off and continued rummaging through the refrigerator.

"Anyway, listen to me baby. You have to be real careful doing those extra curricular activities, because in my days? Many of woman damn near broke their necks. if you catch my drift?" Mrs. Elaine schooled giving Miracle a knowing wink.

"Come on Ma'," Vincent bemoaned as his mother started laughing.

CHAPTER FIVE

Christiana Mall was surprisingly crowded with shoppers as Miracle and Heaven browsed the stores window shopping. It looked like an ant farm from the upper tier aisle as people bustled about below them, meandering along in different directions. It reminded Miracle of a congested highway as she looked down at the bumper to bumper human traffic. The noise sounded like an angry hive of bee's fussing over who's going to get to fuck the queen. Miracle could barely hear Heaven as she shouted above the noise.

"Bitch! I can't believe the niggas mother caught y'all fucking." She laughed as they stood about gossiping at the railing. Miracle rolled her eyes laughing. She still couldn't believe what happened last night.

"She didn't actually catch us in action, but she heard us. And I was embarrassed as shit bitch for real."

"Shit! Hearing is the same fucking thing as getting caught to me. And I can't believe your ass fell into the tub bitch." Heaven snickered as she pictured Miracle sprawled out in the tub with her huger than life naked ass poked high into the air. It was a sight she would of loved to seen as she doubled over from laughter. She couldn't get the image out of her mind.

"Shut the fuck up bitch! Its not funny. A bitch was really stuck in that mother fucker." Miracle scoffed through her own laughter at the unbelievable situation.

Suddenly, there was a commotion right below them and it stole their attention as a large group of females started arguing in the middle of the crowded floor with another pair of girls. People was scattering out of the way trying to avoid the chaotic scene as two of the girls got into a shoving match with each other and Miracle knew it wouldn't be long before a fight broke out.

"Yea, I fucked your nigga bitch and he ate this pussy." One of the girls shouted at the other, while a light-skinned petite girl stood in between them trying to keep them apart.

"Bitch! Fuck you! Your a dirty ass bitch. A ratchet ass hoe and you probably fucked the whole riverside projects too, you nasty ass thot!" The other girl fired back as she tried to reach pass the light-skinned girl to punch the other one.

Miracle looked on stunned. She couldn't believe the shit that was coming out of the young girls mouth. None of them couldn't be no older than fifth-teen years old. *The mouths on these little ass girls is disrespectful!* She thought shaking her head.

"Yo, that little bitch right there is fucking ratchet as shit!" Heaven stated pointing at the young girl that claimed she got her pussy ate. Heaven was enjoying the kitten match.

"Mommy, Mommy are those girls gonna fight?" A seven year old boy asked his mother as she ushered him past the drama.

"Mind your business boy!" The mother scolded and Miracle felt they should be doing the same thing. Minding their own business.

"Heaven come on with your nosy ass. Lets go get something to eat." Miracle suggested snatching Heaven by the hand and half dragging her behind her.

"Damn, I'm coming! Calm your ass down the food ain't going nowhere." Heaven protested fighting to get her hand back as Miracle continued to drag her along.

The food court was packed to capacity and the lines damn near stretched all the way to Macy's. Miracle hated standing in long lines and was pissed, because the longer she stood there waiting the more hungry she felt. But Heaven didn't seem to mind as she stood behind her gossiping on the phone. She was probably talking about those young girls or promoting for some dick. *Damn a bitch is starving!* Miracle thought shuffling on her feet impatiently as the line seemed to dwindle down only an inch at a time.

"Nigga, you gonna get the money...What?...Whatever Aamir, fuck you nigga!" Miracle over heard Heaven saying on the phone. She had no idea who the person was she talking too, because the name didn't sound familiar, but it sounded like she was having a heated discussion.

Miracle glanced over her shoulder at Heaven while she was still bickering on the phone and saw the scowl on her face and wondered about the seriousness of the situation. She was tempted to ask Heaven if everything was alright, but before she had a chance to she already hung up.

"Mother fuckers is something else." Heaven swore, but it was more to herself than to Miracle.

"Your good?" Miracle asked, but more out of curiosity than concern.

"Huh?..Yeah a bitch is good. Just some nigga." She off-handily replied, then fell quiet. Miracle let the subject drop, figuring Heaven would tell whenever she was ready to get it off her perky chest. *Fucking finally!* Miracle thought as she stepped up to the counter of Hibachi's and browsed the menu. She ordered a large platter of chicken and rice with extra sauce and vegetables on the side, while Heaven placed a small order of beef lo mein and a small coke.

After receiving their order, Miracle looked around for a vacant table and found one at the far end of the food court. *Ugh!* She thought as her and Heaven was about to sit down. The table was littered with empty food and drink containers. *Mother fuckers are so disgusting!* Miracle fumed as she cleared the table off and tossed the empty containers into the trash.

"They need to have their workers doing this shit." Miracle complained as she rejoined Heaven back at the table and sat down to dig into her platter.

"Its the mall bitch, get use to it." Heaven sassed playing with her beef lo mein. She really wasn't hungry and lost her appetite after the conversation she had on the phone. Miracle was a totally different story. She was digging into her platter with fervor.

"If your not gonna eat that bitch give it here." Miracle chimed through a mouthful of food as she eyed Heaven's untouched platter. Heaven laughed as she pushed the platter across the table to Miracle.

"Take it with your greedy ass!" Heaven teased and started laughing when Miracle stuck out her tongue with chewed up food still on it. Miracle laughed and finished off both platters of food before they continued window shopping through the mall.

The department store Macy's was having a half-off sale on their merchandise and Heaven wanted to stop inside to see what kind of deals they had on clothes. As Heaven browsed the crowded aisles looking at the racks of jeans on sale, Miracle decided to check out the lingerie section. She wanted to find something cute and sexy to wear for Vincent, even though she already owned a bunch of different colored laced Veronica Ann negligees. *Damn! Do they even got a bitch's size in here?* She thought sifting through the labels.

Miracle was so occupied looking for the right size to squeeze her big ass into, she didn't notice as a male sales clerk slid up beside her.

"I think you would look beautiful in this piece right here, even the color matches your beauty." The clerk seduced holding a two-piece pink Victoria Secret negligee up to her body. Miracle looked at him with a cross expression on her face. His words sounded flattering but she was too fat to know better.

"Excuse me?" She asked peevishly and was ready to give him a piece of her mind, until she heard a bunch of laughter coming from the next aisle.

"Ugh! You see that fat nasty bitch over there trying to look sexy? She's gonna look a big ass walrus squeezed into a Tutu." A female cracked to the applause of laughter. It was the same group of young girls that were arguing earlier.

Instantly, Miracle felt embarrassed by the insult as her body-consciousness came to the surface. She was furious as she stared at the mocking teens and started to retaliate with her own comeback, but Heaven's response was quicker.

"Who the fuck you think your talking too? I'll beat your little young ass bitch!" Heaven threatened as she confronted the group of girls. Miracle wasn't surprised by

Heaven's aggressive outburst, because she knew her bestie was more brazen than a bottle of Patron. The group of girls turned in Heaven's direction as she approached them and the whole store fell under a suspense hush.

"Um..What?.. Who are you talking too? I wasn't talking about you." The girl stated with a false bravado as Heaven stepped close in her face.

"I'm talking to you bitch! I will drag you all through this mother fucking store and think I'm playing bitch. Say something else slick about my sister and watch me pull that raggedy ass weave out of your head." Heaven promised with a finger pointing threateningly in the young girls face.

The girls eyes widened with nervousness as she looked to her friends for confidence but found none as they stared back at her in stunned silence. None of them wanted any parts of Heaven. Once the reality of her situation sunk in and she realized her friends wasn't coming to her aid, the young girl tucked her tail and made a hasty retreat for the exit.

"That's what I thought bitch!-" Heaven shouted at her retreating back, then turned and addressed the sales clerk.

"-And she 'll take that negligee in black please." she declared.

CHAPTER SIX

"Vincent!, Vincent! Boy I know you hear me calling your narrow behind." His mother yelled upstairs as she stood at the bottom of the landing. *That damn boy act like he's hard of hearing.* She thought walking back into the living room as she heard his loud foot falls descending the stairs. Mrs. Elaine had been wanting to have a heart to heart talk with her son for awhile now, but she had barely seen or spoken to him ever since he's been so busy stuck up that girl's ass. It wasn't that she had a problem with him spending so much time with Miracle, because it was far from the truth. she had a strong motherly fondness for her and thought it would finally do Vincent some good to be in a committed relationship for a change. But it was the commitment part on his end that concerned her.

"Yea ma, whats good?" He asked as he plopped down on the sofa across from her. He could tell something was on her mind, because she had a certain look on her face and it was never a good sign. *Here we go.* He thought as he prepared himself for the bullshit.

"Vincent, I am not trying to control what you do in your life or tell you what to do understand? But Miracle is a sweet girl and she really is in-love with you and I hope your not stringing that girl along and playing with her heart as you have done so many times with these other girls.-" Vincent was about to start protesting, but Mrs. Elaine held a finger up to silence him.

"-Wait, just listen. I am not saying that's what your doing, I am hoping your not doing that. Because that girl has been through a lot in her life and don't need you adding any of your nonsense along with it. I know you can be just like your father and you done showed that many times in the past. And I am not saying this to hurt you boy, because I love you. But I don't want you to hurt that girl because it will devastate her understand me? So if you don't love her Vincent you need to sit her down and tell her the truth, because she do deserve to know. You have seen all the bullshit your father put me through and Lord knows I loved that man and put up with all kind nonsense. The constant cheating with other woman and the lying, boy it took a heavy toll on me. It almost broke me completely if it wasn't for the Lord. But I put on a brave face for everyone and stayed strong until I didn't have any more strength left in me. Its why I suffered from that nervous break-down and ended up in the hospital-" Mrs. Elaine fell into a quiet reflection for a moment before she started speaking again.

"-I just want you to be the kind of man your father never could be. Do you understand me Vincent?" She expressed with a heavy heart.

"Ma, I do understand. And you don't have to worry about me being unfaithful and untrue like my father, because I am nothing like him. I really do love Miracle and I know she is the one for me. So I will never cheat on her because I know she been through a lot in her life and I never want to be the one to hurt her, only love her and to show her that in every way possible." He assured her with a smile on his handsome face as he gave her a hug.

"Are you seeing her today?" She asked.

"Yea, she is suppose to be coming by my house later on this evening. Why what's up?" Vincent asked guarded. He couldn't never be sure what was coming next with his mother.

Mrs. Elaine laughed, because She knew her son well and knew he thought she was up to something.

"Boy, relax yourself. I just wanted you to tell her I said hello and she need to come spend sometime with her mama." Mrs. Elaine said, then slippery added.

"And I need you to run to Walmart for me." Vincent sighed, shaking his with a laugh. He knew she was up to something.

"I figured you was buttering me up for something lady." He said laughing as his mother fished the money out of her purse and he fast peddled out of the front door before she could give him another errand to run.

****

Miracle wasn't feeling well as she sat on the toilet again for the third time in the past twenty-minutes. Her stomach was killing her and she hoped she wasn't coming down with a stomach virus, because she had the runs every since she left the mall earlier with Heaven. It had to come from the food she ate while at Hibachi's. *Oh my fucking God!* She thought wrapping her arms snugly around her mid-section trying to lessen the cramping pain in her stomach as she let loose a loud fart and a murky down pour of diarrhea splashed forcefully into the toilet. *Ugh!* She thought with disgust as the murky wetness back splashed onto her butt. *A bitch definitely got to get in the shower!* She thought aggravatingly as another waterfall gushed out of her bowls. Her asshole was red-raw and burning.

After shitting out a five-gallon bucket of spoiled chitterlings, at least from the smell of things, miracle stripped out of her clothes and climbed into the shower trying to scrub away the stench of shit that clung to her body. *I hope a bitch is feeling better by the time I see Vincent tonight.* She brooded as she toweled off and marched her naked stinging ass into the bedroom. She had moved quickly on her feet, because the friction caused by her huge ass-cheeks rubbing only intensified the stinging as she walked. Miracle bathed in the sweet-smelling fragrance of Warm Vanilla lotion and made sure she put a dab of A&D ointment on raw asshole. *It feel like a bitch got fucked in her ass.* She thought smiling at the nasty memory.

Miracle finished getting dressed and sprawled across the bed in the fetus position, because she didn't want to apply pressure to her stomach or sore ass cheeks. She wasn't even trying to breathe hard, because she feared it would cause her to shit on herself And that was something she couldn't afford to do. As she gently rocked herself from side to side hoping to settle the bubbling inside of her stomach, her phone rang. It was Heaven as expected.

"Hello?" She groaned in a hoarse voice that sounded constipated.

"Damn bitch! You sound like your taking shit. What's the matter with you?" Heaven teased in her usual playful manner.

"I feel like shit and that's all a bitch been doing all day. I have the fucking runs. A bitch's stomach is bubbling even now as we speak." Miracle complained as she tentatively scooted to the edge of the bed and immediately regret it as she farted. It sounded like a muffled whistle blown with spittle as it swooshed out of her.

"Your probably coming down with a stomach virus or the shit could of came from that nasty ass food you ate in the mall today. And speaking of the mall, guess who the fuck I saw walking on the East side? That little bitch from the mall. I was about to jump out of my car on that bitch, but she looked shook when she realized it was me. Oh shit! wasn't you suppose to be seeing Vincent tonight? Heaven Remembered.

"Yea, that was the plans we made, but I might have to cancel if my stomach keeps acting up. I ain't trying to be running back and forth to the bathroom all night at his house. That shit is embarrassing. But I really don't want to stand him up either." Miracle confessed and heaven could tell she was weighing her options. But one thing was definitely for certain, it didn't weigh as much as she did.

"Well, if you really want to go? Then go fuck it. Just make sure your ass wear a pamper." Heaven joked and got the wrong response as she heard Miracle shout *'Holy shit!'* then the sound of heavy feet pounding on the floor.

"Miracle! Miracle! Are you alright?" Heaven yelled into the phone concerned. *What the fuck is going on?* She thought listening to the commotion in the background, until the unmistakable sound of diarrhea hitting water resounded with a loud splash. It sounded like someone poured a bucket of water into the toilet.

"Ugh! Oh my God bitch I know your nasty ass is not shitting?" Heaven snapped through fits of laughter.

"Shut up bitch its not funny. Hang up the phone." Miracle demanded. She had forgot the phone was on speaker when she rushed into the bathroom and dropped it on the floor in her haste to reach the toilet.

"Bye shitty!" Heaven punted and hung up laughing. After refreshing and changing her clothes, Miracle decided to throw caution to the wind and go ahead with her plans to meet Vincent at his house. Because she knew first hand how it felt to be stood up, very hurtful and she didn't want to be the cause of his pain.

Miracle parked her rust-colored Honda Accord at the corner of 28th & Washington street and walked a half of block down to Vincent's house. She was surprised to see the block wasn't flooded with a bunch of rowdy ass niggas and ratchet bitches posted like stop signs on the corner as she climbed his porch and knocked on the front door. *I know this nigga is in the house and hear me knocking!* She thought with a growing frustration as she stared at his Chevy Capri parked out front. *I know this nigga is not standing me up after I came all the way over here? Sick and all!* Her questioning thoughts ran rampant through her mind as she started to feel the familiar pain from her past. *Why did he do this to me?* She wondered as she spun on her heels ready to leave until the front door swung open.

"Hey beautiful, you leaving already? You just got here." Vincent crooned with a seductive smile as he gave her a tender kiss on the lips. Miracle felt the tight grip around her heart loosen as she hugged him tight. *Oh my God! He didn't stand me up.* She thought with a prayerful relief.

"I-I thought..." She started to say, but couldn't get the words out.

"What? You thought I stood you up didn't you? I would never do that to you beautiful. It took me long to answer the door because I have a surprise for you and wasn't done setting it up yet when you knocked on the door." Vincent explained as he led her into the house. *A surprise?*

What kind of surprise do he got for me? She thought in wonder as Vincent made her close her eyes.

Miracle was filled with a child's wonder as he guided her by the hand inside and when he told her to open her eyes, her mouth dropped open in stunned shock. She couldn't believe what she was seeing and broke down into an emotional mess. There was beautiful assorted rose pedals scattered about the floor, leading to a candle lit dinning table with a bottle of red wine on ice and the savory aroma of cooked steak in the air. It looked so romantically beautiful. Miracle was moved beyond words.

"Its all for you beautiful. I hope you like it." He stated watching her shocked reaction. *Like it? I fucking love it.* She thought feeling something inexpressible inside, because never in a millions years would she have thought a man would do something so romantic for her.

"Oh my God Vincent! I love it and I love you so fucking much. Thank you." She cried passionately with tears running down her dark face.

"Anything for my beautiful lady. I love you more." He seduced kissing away her tears and leading her over to the table, where he pulled out the chair for her to sit down. Miracle melted inside. It was the first time he said he loved her.

"And I hope you brought your appetite with you beautiful." he added disappearing into the kitchen and returned carrying two plates.

Vincent had sat the delicious smelling plate of food in front of Miracle, then took his place at the opposite end of the table and popped open the bottle of the wine. *Oh my God! I hope my stomach don't start acting up, especially after all he done went through to make this happen.*

Miracle thought sizing up the tasty looking steak as he filled their glasses with the red wine.

"I hope you don't mind drinking Pinot Noir? It was the only thing I could grab in short notice." Vincent said apologetically. *Nigga a bitch would drink water as long as its with you!* Miracle thought but didn't express it.

"I really don't mind. Its fine with me." She reassured him as they ate in ambient glow of the candle light. It was close to mid-night by the time they finished eating and decided to retire to the bedroom for the night. Miracle felt stuffed and was thankful she didn't have to continuously run back and forth to the bathroom during dinner. As Vincent cleared the empty plates off the table, she relaxed as her food settled and waited on him to get done.

Miracle started feeling the strong urge of lust burning hot between her legs as she trailed behind Vincent like a shadow towards the bedroom and each step she took closer to the room only intensified the anticipation. She couldn't wait to feel him deep inside of her. Vincent opened the bedroom door and Miracle almost fainted from shock. The bedroom was decorated even more extravagantly than the down stairs living room. It looked like a newlywed lovers suite on their honey moon at the Waldorf Astoria Hotel in New York City. Miracle felt weak in the knees and not just from the romantic view of the room. Her mouth watered for more than food this time as she pushed Vincent into the bedroom and started to drop down onto her knees before him.

But suddenly, there was a loud bang like the sound of a truck back firing and Miracle froze as her bowls released a horrific gaseous fart. And immediately, She felt the thick murky wetness smear the inside of her thighs. *Ooh my fucking God!* She thought mortified as she knelt half squatted in front of him and the smell even made it worse. *What the fuck?* Vincent thought trying to hold back his laughter as he reached down to lift her up. But Miracle refused to move. It was the most embarrassing moment in her life. Inside, she had felt like dying so she wouldn't have to face the humiliation and shame of her shitting on herself in front of the one person in the world who's opinion mattered.

"Hey, look at me beautiful. Its going to be alright don't worry." Vincent assured her in a soothing tone. But Miracles mind was too far away to hear him. *Beautiful? There ain't nothing beautiful about me. I am a fucking pathetic ugly mess.* She thought pitifully as Vincent's lifted her onto her feet and slowly guided her into the bathroom. The moisture squished between her thick thighs as she walked and she wondered if he could hear the slushy wetness.

"I got you beautiful." Vincent consoled as he turned on the hot water and quickly stripped Miracle out of her soiled clothes and helped her into the shower.

Miracle felt ashamed as she stood fully exposed in the shower with her limbs out stretched like a child as Vincent gently washed every inch of her body and after he was done he made passionate love to her under the warm spray of the shower.

CHAPTER SEVEN

"Bitch! Where the fuck have you been hiding at for the past couple of days? I've been blowing your fucking phone up like a stalker and your ass still didn't call a bitch back. What the fuck is going on with you?" Heaven angrily fussed as soon as Miracle opened the front door and she stormed inside. Miracle haven't been herself lately ever since the mishap took place at Vincent's house and secluded herself like a hermit trying to regain some measure of self-respect back. Not even Vincent was able to break through the wall of her self-loathing.

"I just been going through something and haven't been in the mood to really be bothered. A bitch been stressed out for real." Miracle replied as she crawled back onto the sofa and told Heaven everything that happened.

"Get the fuck out of here! Are you serious? Oh my God! A bitch would of died on the spot for real. So what is Vincent talking about?" Heaven asked in a state of disbelief. She couldn't believe Miracle actually shitted on herself in front of him and what made the shit even worse, she was about to give the nigga some sloppy top.

"He seems fine with the situation. But I can't even look the nigga in his eyes without feeling some kind of way. I keep thinking he's looking at me differently since it happened and he's just not trying to hurt a bitch's feeling." Miracle explained.

"Bitch! Your tripping for real. Why would you even think that? The nigga washed you up and still made love to you in the shower. What nigga you know would of done that? I don't even know a nigga that would of done some shit like that for real. Another nigga would of been quick to clown a bitch and kicked your ass out of their house. The nigga must really love you." Heaven remarked with honesty.

"Yea, maybe your right. A bitch might be tripping." Miracle agreed thoughtfully.

Heaven stood up and started rummaging through her jeans pocket looking for the quarter ounce of weed she brought to smoke as Miracle sat lost staring at the television.

"This shit right here is some fire bitch! I couldn't even smoke a whole blunt to the face by myself, that's how high a bitch was for real." Heaven stressed rolling up a blunt of the good-good and wrapping her lips around the brown stick as she sparked it. She took an exaggerated long pull on the blunt, filling her lungs and blew the pungent smelling smoke into the air.

"Damn bitch! That shit is strong." Miracle quipped with her nose scrunched up as the stench of the weed permeated the air. Heaven laughed feeling the immediate effects of the weeds potent intoxication.

"You gotta hit this bitch." Heaven drawled passing the blunt to her.

Miracle sucked hard on the blunt inhaling deeply and immediately started coughing as the thick bluish smoke snaked down her throat and caused her eyes to water. Heaven started laughing belligerently and didn't know if came from being so high or from seeing Miracle choking on the weed.

"B-bitch! What is so funny? This shit is strong as fuck, a bitch almost died. What the fuck is this?" Miracle coughed as she passed the blunt back to Heaven.

"I don't know bitch. But whatever its called? It can definitely get this heavenly pussy anytime, because a bitch is higher than a mother fucker and ready to get fuck." Heaven jestered with a throaty laugh.

"Bitch you are a hot mess." Miracle said chuckling along with her.

"But seriously, if you would of taken my advice in the beginning? You wouldn't been in that situation." Heaven advised suddenly changing the topic of the discussion. Miracle was lost. *What is this high bitch talking about?* She thought staring at Heaven with a dumb founded expression on her face.

"What? What the hell are you talking about now?" Miracle questioned.

"If your ass would of wore that pamper like I told you to that night? Then a bitch would've of been good ya hear me?" Heaven counseled refreshing Miracles memory as she sucked down another pull on the blunt. *Oh no this high ass bitch didn't just go there?* Miracle thought and was about to verbally dig into Heaven's ass, but her phone rang.

"Hold that thought bitch!" Miracle shot at Heaven as she reached and answered the phone.

"Hello?"

"Hey beautiful. How are you feeling?" Vincent inquired. He was sincerely worried about her.

"I am feeling better and I'm sorry I've been a little distant towards you. I hope you can forgive me and understand." Miracle apologized and tried to stifle her laugh as she watched Heaven making smoochy faces at her.

"You okay?" Vincent asked hearing the muffled snicker.

"Yea babe I'm good. Just sitting here with Heavens crazy ass smoking on some chow." Miracle said through a haze of smoke.

"So the reason I called is tell you we going out tonight and I am not taking no for an answer understand? So get your beautiful self dolled up and make sure you wear a dress alright? And tell Heaven I said what's up." Vincent declared and hung up before she had a chance to protest.

Miracle shook her with laugh at Vincent's audaciousness as she swiveled her head and looked back at Heaven.

"Now! Back to you bitch with your slick ass mouth." Miracle fired.

****

Later that evening, Miracle had picked out the perfect attire to wear as she two-step happily around the bedroom while getting ready. It was a red strapless Veronica Ann dress with matching pumps. *A bitch is gonna look good in this!* She thought, holding the dress up to her body in front of the full-length mirror. Miracle had loved the dress and never thought she would get a chance to wear it until now. She squeezed every inch of her voluptuous plump figure into the dress and admired her reflection in the mirror. It fitted her with perfection and hugged every curve of her roundness. She looked amazing.

Miracle was feeling a lot like her usual self or maybe she was still high from the weed she smoked earlier with

Heaven, whichever the case, she was looking forward to having a good time.

"Beautiful are you ready to go?" Vincent shouted from downstairs as he waited in the living room. He was eagerly impatient and couldn't wait to see the expression on her face when he showed her the surprise he had in store for her.

"Yea babe I'm coming now!" She yelled back taking a second look at herself mirror to make sure nothing was out of place. She looked fat-tastic. As Miracle quickly sashayed downstairs, Vincent was waiting at the bottom of the steps with a tantalizing smile on his face and a mischievous look in his eyes.

"Wow! You definitely look beautiful in that dress baby." He admired taking her by the hand and twirling her around. Miracle blushed like a high school preteen. *Damn! This nigga always know what to say to a bitch to get her panties wet.* She thought as her kitty purred in agreement.

"Thanks you babe. I always wanted to wear this dress but never had nowhere to go special in it. Is everything all set?" She asked eager to find out what he had awaiting for her.

"Yea, everything is all good. the reservations is set. But there is one small thing left to do." He said with a mistrusting serpentine smile on his handsome face as he handed her a velvet box. *I know this ain't what I think it is? A ring? Is this nigga gonna propose to me?* A million questions ran through her mind.

"Ooh my God! Vincent!" Miracle gushed with elation as her trembling fingers quickly unwrapped the red ribbon and she sprung open the box. Miracle gasped! With a shocked, but amused expression on her face.

"Really baby?" She breathed as he stood there with a wickedly grin on his face.

"You are the fuck something else nigga." She said removing the item from the box and examining it as a curious stirring brewed deep within her.

It was a custom made silicon based five-speed remote controlled vibrator with an attachment that stimulated the clitoris. It was designed to insert inside of the vagina comfortably. Vincent had it shipped in for the special occasion.

"Now run your beautiful self back upstairs and put that in and don't wear any panties." Vincent instructed. Miracle's dark round cheeks almost turned the color of her dress as she quickly turned and ascended the stairs. It didn't take long for her to come back downstairs wearing a smile on her face and with an anticipating throbbing between her legs as Vincent escorted her out of the house and into his waiting Chevy Capri. Miracle sat with a quiet expectation as she gazed out the window at the bright lights of the city Wilmington as they drove the on I-95 expressway. It was a beautiful sight and looked like every other major City in the States. Even with its crime infested hoods. Miracle peeked over at Vincent's handsome face as he drove and was so grateful she met a man like him.

After a twenty-minute drive, the Chevy Capri came to a slow stop and parked in front of The Melting Pot restaurant. It was an elegant Five-star restaurant that catered to the have's and have's not of Wilmington, so obtaining a reservation wasn't an issue. Miracle stepped out of the car into the warm night air feeling like a Diva and she definitely looked the part as the host greeted them at the entrance like royalty.

"Mr. and Mrs. Vincent its a pleasure to have you this evening. Please follow me." The sharply dress host greeted as he led them to their awaiting table. Miracle was all smile and wasn't use to that kind of service as Vincent winked at the host knowing it wasn't in his job description. It was the reason he secretly coated his pockets ahead of time.

"Some one will be here shortly to take your orders." He informed them as he disappeared to attend to other patrons.

The restaurant was pleasantly crowded with a mixture of different ethnicity's and the atmosphere was alive with the small chatter of voices and ambient music playing softly in the background.

"It is so beautiful in here Vincent. How in the world did you find this place? I been living here all my life and never knew this restaurant existed. And you know how much a bitch love food." Miracle whispered in a low tone as she looked around at the many shades of people in the restaurant. Vincent chuckled.

"I can't divulge all my secrets in one night beautiful." He crooned playfully with a fox's sly grin on his face as he watched happiness dancing in her eyes. He was glad to see she was back from the nightmare of her humiliation and fully awake in the reality of her normal self. Miracle laughed. It was a throaty laugh and full of sexual tenor.

"So, are you gonna tell me the workings of this devise I have secretly implanted in my curious kitty?" She asked whispering in a conspirator tone across the table.

"In due time beautiful. In due time." Vincent replied evasively and his remark only heightened her anticipation as the stirring between her legs intensified. *Oh my God!*

This niggas playing hard to get! She thought as her mind swam in an ocean of curiosity.

Miracle knew it was useless trying to pry the information out of him, because at times he could be as stubborn as a rusty hinge. So she concentrated her attention on the menu trying to ignore the crackling fire sparking out of control between her thighs as a waiter suddenly appeared at their table.

"Good evening. Are you ready to place y'all order?" He asked with his pen poised and ready to scribble down their order. It was at the exact moment Vincent decided to removed the wireless remote control out of his pocket and switched it on. Miracle gasped with a jolt as vibrating tendrils sent a stream of small current passing through her body and the waiter became immediately concerned as he looked at her.

"Are you alright Ma'am?" He asked wondering if she needed a drink of water because she looked flustered. Miracle was beyond flustered.

"No, no I am okay. Thank you." She affirmed to the waiter as she looked over at a smiling Vincent. He had a look of enjoyment on his face. *Oh! This niggas gonna get it tonight.* She thought with a smile on her face.

"We are good for now. Just bring us a bottle of your finest red wines please." Vincent addressed the waiter as he kept his smiling eyes glued on Miracle. The waiter disappeared.

"Oh my fucking God Vincent Really? This is how you wanna play I see. Alright you got it for now" Miracle stated playfully with a hidden threat in her words. Vincent laughed as he watched her recovering from the ordeal.

"Don't worry beautiful, it's only the beginning. Lets see what the rest of the evening will have in store for you" He forewarned and she flicked him the middle finger. She could only imagine. Vincent had only given her a small taste of the pleasure and didn't want to overwhelm her, at least not yet, because the night was still young.

The waiter had returned carrying a fresh bottle of Chianti, an Italian red wine, and filled their glasses and quickly disappeared, leaving the bottle in a chilled bucket of ice on the table. Miracle and Vincent had engaged in small chatter about the mundane politics of the hood as they sipped on the delicious red wine and savored its flavoring taste.

"Yea, you could never be too careful on the North side.." Vincent was saying as he looked at Miracle over the rim of his glass with a salacious smile on his face. His lustful gaze conveyed his intentions as he set the controls on the remote to level two and pressed the button. Miracle's body immediately came to attention as synaptic charges of pleasure shot through her vaginal region and she stifled a soft moan that was attempting to escape out of mouth as her body hummed from the surging pleasure.

She had squeezed her legs tightly together and tried to contain the fire burning hotly inside of her as her clit singed with ecstasy like a flaming candle.

"Vincent!" She murmured softly as she sat helplessly caught in the throes of lust and he ignored her plea as he basked in her pleasurable suffering and cruelly brought her to the next level.

"Ooh God!" She uttered loudly gripping the edges of the table as a punishing and unforgiving slash of pleasure cut through her entire body. It was merciless... tormenting her clitoris like the licks of a thousand tongues. She felt dizzy with wanton.

"Tell me you want more." Vincent taunted with a salacious cruelness in his voice.

"No, No...No More." She whimpered biting down hard on her red coated bottom lip.

Patrons at the nearest tables stole fugitive glances at Miracle and wondered about her peculiar behavior. Vincent nonchalantly ignored their gaze and took a long sip of his red wine as he watched her like a cat toying with a mice.

"P-l-e-a-s-e babe!" She stuttered with a quiver in her voice as her eyes pleaded for mercy. But she found no solace as Vincent intensified the level of affliction and her body jerked hard like she was struck by the tongs of a whip as a bolt of lightening pleasure slashed through her pulsating clit. Miracle trembled clutching between her thighs as the fiery pleasure coursed through the core of her vagina.

"Ooh!...Fuck!" She shrieked drowning in the sweet abyss of pleasure and her loud moan drew the eyes of other patrons at surrounding tables. Most of them thought she was having a seizure and was confused by Vincent's calm demeanor as he smiled reassuringly at the onlookers hoping to assuage their curiosity as an earth shattering orgasm held Miracle captive in its embrace.

The intensive pulsating vibrations of the vibrator were relentless like a million Nanomites was tickling on her clit. The feeling was unimaginably euphoric and beads of sweat trickled down the edges of her temple as the heat from her cunt rose within her like a cremating furnace. Suddenly, the waiter re- appeared at the table with his pen poised to take their order and Vincent showed her a measure of mercy as he gave her a small reprieve from her anguish. It was like a refreshing cold glass of water in her hellish pleasure and she was fraught with thirst. But not the kind from drinking.

The waiter had a stern look of concern on his face as he inadvertently gazed at Miracle's disheveled appearance.

"Are you ready to order now, Mr. and Mrs. Vincent" He asked with a polite courtesy trying not to stare at Miracle's flustered face. She looked disheveled.

"Definitely. I am starving right about now. How about you beautiful?" Vincent asked smiling beguilingly at Miracle. She looked at him for a long moment through haze filled eyes before she responded.

"I-I am st-starved." She stuttered trying to compose herself as she reached for her glass of wine with a shaky hand and was grateful Vincent had refilled her drink. She could still feel the subtle pulse of her throbbing clit as it drummed between her trembling legs. Vincent ordered the house's special for the both of them.

"So, beautiful how are you feeling? I hope you are enjoying it as much me." He said after the waiter had disappeared to fetch their meal. There was a colorful hint of playful sarcasm in his voice.

"Baby why are you doing this to me? I could barely hold myself together and where out here in public. I am so fucking horny and my pussy is so wet! I think I stained the whole back of my dress." She confided feeling a smudge of embarrassment, but yet, She felt dirty and sluttish.

The waiter had swiftly returned back to the table carrying a tray of; Parmesan Risotto with Roasted Shrimp and a fresh bottle of Chianti, and quickly disappeared. Miracle wasted no time digging into her food with fervor as they ate in quiet fortitude. Miracle's body had felt replenished after burning off the calories between her legs and the color returned to her face.

"Um..Baby. This food is delicious." She expressed, taking the last bite and chasing it down with a swallow of wine. Vincent had agreed as he finished off his plate and dabbed his mouth with a napkin.

"I can not wait until we get home baby I..." Miracle's words trailed off and she had a lewd tint in her eyes as lick her succulent lips.

Vincent smirked sordidly as he reached under the table and triggered the remote control settings on the highest frequency. Miracle was caught unaware and Jumped as a flash of blinding voltage scourged her clit. It had felt like billions of gentle tiny pin pricks dancing on her clitoris as a low subtle whine could be heard buzzing between her legs like a multitude of whispering bees.

"Ooh!...Ooh!...Ooh!" Miracle moaned clutching her stomach as a churning tornado of thunderous pleasure seized her. The sensation was intense. She could feel it in her asshole as it speared her cunt and stabbed every nerve ending in her clit. It was a sweet painful pleasure.

"Ah!...Ooh God!" Miracle bucked in her seat shivering as a river of wetness trickled down her legs and pooled in her shoes.

"Ooh!...Ooh!...Ooh my fucking God!" She cried out as her face morphed into a mask of sexual torment as tidal waves of orgasm's relentlessly washed over her and threatened to drown her in the depths of unforgiving pleasure.

Miracle trembled intensely as Vincent smiled wickedly watching her writhe in her seat inconsolably. Other Patrons gasped! Shocked and confused watching as she clutch her stomach and wondered if she was in the throes of some kind sickness as they looked on with concern eyes.

"Oh My!" A few woman whispered aghast, recognizing the tell-tale signs of an orgasm. Miracle cupped at her large breast and slipped a hand down in-between her thighs and palmed her throbbing crotch as she gyrated against the seat. A pungent musky scent had permeated the air and mixed with the aroma's of the food. It was intoxicating and Vincent savored the sweet scented smell of her juices.

"Good God!" an elderly gentlemen with graying hair bellowed as he watched her make love to an imaginary lover while another man was sitting at the table. Miracle couldn't take it no more as her stomach muscles tightened and her cunt contracted violently as the savage spasms of an orgasm over taken her. She tipped her back and moaned loudly. The guttural cry echoed through out the restaurant bouncing off the walls like a high pitch frequency ball.

Many of the patrons in the restaurant frantically waved down the host and pointed to the unruly table of Miracle and Vincent as he started easing her out of the euphoric state she was suspended in.

"Is everything alright over here?" The host asked concerned as he stared at Miracle. She looked drained and disarrayed. Her perfectly straightened hair was disheveled and sweated out as she slightly twitched with a dazed expression on her face. Vincent chuckled heartily at the host.

"Yea we are definitely good and to be honest? everything is perfect." He replied to the host as he smiled at Miracle.

"I fucking love you" She stammered breathlessly with a weak smile on her face and a satisfied gleam in her eye as

Vincent laughed. After returning home Vincent fucked her until the sun came up.

CHAPTER EIGHT

Miracle's morning was slowly dragging along like a nigga without legs and she was exhausted as the hours seemed to stretch into eternity. It only had been a week since she returned back to work and already she was looking forward to her next vacation. *A bitch should of used all of her sick days.* She thought as she sat bored behind her desk and daydreamed of Vincent, while doodling on a piece of paper. There wasn't anything to do around the office besides paper work and even that was close to nothing. It was a dramatically slow day and working as an insurance agent in a relatively small and unknown company was like sitting around a nursing home eating jelly with senor citizens.

There was only two other females besides herself and a male employee that worked at Regal Insurance. She had been working for the company since it first opened about a year ago and wanted to quit for even longer, because the hours she was putting in wasn't matching her pay check. But a dollar beats a blank. It was something her foster parent use to say. And besides, she had bills that needed to be attended too like every other tax paying citizen.

As she started shuffling through a pile of files on her desk looking for a certain case number, the office building door swung open and a deliver guy waltz inside carrying a bouquet of flowers. Everybody froze.

"Is there a Ms. Miracle Walters here?" He asked looking around the small office at the employee's as curious eyes stared back at him. At first nobody spoke, then a pale looking female pointed to the back of the office at Miracle.

"These are for you Ma'am." He said and exited as suddenly as he came.

Miracle opened the card that was attached to the bouquet of beautiful roses and her eyes started to tear up as she read the words that were written:

'To my most beautiful love Miracle.
I hope these brighten your day
as you have brighten my world.
With all the love in my heart!
Love Vincent.

She couldn't stop smiling as she cradled the flowers against her chest and inhaled deeply, smelling the refreshing fragrance of the roses. *Oh my God! I love this nigga so much!* She thought happily in love and was unaware of the curious eyes watching her.

"Miracle?..Miracle?" Kimberly called in a loud whisper as she fanned her hand trying to get Miracle's attention. Kimberly was one of the other female employees. She was a petite blonde with blue eyes and perky breast. Miracle had never like her because she acted conceited and stuck up at times.

"Huh?..Oh hey whats up Kim?" Miracle cheesed opening her eyes after hearing Kim calling her name.

"Who are they from girl?" She asked with a smiling curiosity. Miracle could tell her fake smile wasn't a friendly one and the bitch was just trying to gather information with her nosy ass. She was the office's despot.

"Who else would be sending me roses but my man." Miracle adduced with spice of sarcasm in her tone.

"Oh! That's nice." Kimberly extolled weakly, flashing her a smile that was more counterfeit than an Instagram model's ass. *Fat bitch!* Kimberly thought as she went back to doing nothing.

"Thank you." Miracle flung, wishing her words could knock the shit out of Kimberly. *Skinny ass bitch!* She thought, pushing Kimberly to the back of her mind and went back to daydreaming about Vincent.

The afternoon couldn't come fast enough for Miracle as she impatiently watched the clock wishing twelve-thirty would hurry up and come so she could go on lunch break. She was starving. *A bitch need a snack or something.* She thought as her stomach rumbled harder than an underground brawl. *Shit! The next time I'm gonna let his ass know to send a bitch a platter of food instead of roses.* She laughed to herself as a medium height, middle age looking dark-skinned man with a fresh out of the pen muscular- build entered the office and headed straight in her direction. All eyes were on her immediately. Especially Kimberly's.

"Hi, how are you doing today sir? How can I help you?" Miracle greeted cheerfully and didn't receive an immediate response as the man stood there staring intensely at her. *Please! don't tell me I got a fucking nut job.* She thought with growing agitation.

"Miracle?" The stranger said, but it was more like a question of uncertainty.

"Yes, may I help you with something sir?" Miracle repeated. The stranger just smiled at her and there was a fondness in his eyes. *Yea! This mother fucker is definitely a wack job.* She thought with conclusion.

"Um..I have been looking for you a long time Miracle. And now I've finally found you. Look at you? Your so beautiful and-"

"Excuse me? But do I know you sir? And what do you mean you've been looking for me a long time?" She rudely asked, interrupting him in mid-sentence.

Miracle was trying to keep her composure because she was at work. *I know this crazy mother fucker is not some kind of stalker. Now that I finally got a man, nigga's want to come out of the wood works? Why the fuck is he looking for me?* She pondered and was ready to give him a piece of her uncensored mind.

"Hold on, hold on maybe I came off the wrong way at first and gave you the wrong impression. My name is Benjamin Miracle. Benjamin Walters and I am your father." The stranger confessed and she thought her world suddenly came to a stop as his words dropped on her like a nuclear bomb and her mind exploded into a billion pieces of disbelief.

"What?" She hissed, feeling like she stepped into an episode of the Twilight Zone. She couldn't believe what she heard and stared at him like he sprouted two heads. The entire office fell under a deaf-mute's silence as everyone focused their attention on her conversation.

"Listen, I know this is a lot to drop on your lap at once and I am truly sorry, but we really need to talk Miracle. I know you a lot of questions on your mind and I am hear to answer all of them understand? So here is my number to reach me in case you want to talk. And again I'm sorry to come to your job like this out of the blue. But it was the only way I could find you." Benjamin explained and slowly spun on heels to leave the office. *Questions? Mother fucker I've been having questions since a baby.* Miracle thought as she watched him walking towards the exit door.

"Wait!-" Miracle shouted after him as she came from behind the desk and caught up with him. "-I have a break in like fifteen-minutes. We can talk then okay?" She suggested and he smiled his agreement.

CHAPTER NINE

Miracle couldn't believe she had finally met her father after so many years of being absence in her life. Or at least the man claiming to be her biological father. She still couldn't wrap her mind around it as she walked throughout the house in a daze straightening up imaginary filth. Even though it was already tidy and spotless. She had invited Benjamin over to the house for a brief visit so they could talk more privately, but she was having second thoughts now as her mind ran rampantly unchecked with doubtfulness. *How the fuck do I even know if he is my real father? I don't look like him and he damn sure don't look nothing like me. And why am I just finding out his name after twenty-nine fucking years?* Miracle couldn't stop the bombardment of questioning thoughts as they violently assaulted her mind.

She was tempted to call her so-called father and let him know she changed her mind and didn't want to talk or to be bothered with him, but something wouldn't let her do it as she swept over the same spot on the floor twice. *Just give the man a chance to explain. It's the least you can do.* A good part of her thought and she was about to start arguing with herself until her phone rang. *Maybe its him calling to say he can't make it, just like he couldn't make any other day in my life.* She thought as she answered the phone.

"Hello?"

"Why your ass didn't call me when you got off work bitch?" Heaven snapped as soon as she answered the phone.

"My bad girl, I meant to but it slipped my mind for real. I had the most unexpected person come into my job today and you wouldn't believe in a million fucking years who that someone happened to be bitch?...My mother fucking daddy!"

"What bitch?..Your daddy? Who the nigga Vincent?" Heaven asked dumbfounded and Miracle laughed at her stupidity.

"No bitch, not Vincent. Even though the nigga is my daddy. But a bitch's biological father." Miracle clarified for Heaven's simple-minded ass.

"Get the fuck out of here bitch! Are you fucking serious?" Heaven shrieked with incredulity.

"Yes bitch! I'm more serious than a bitch needing to lose weight. I couldn't fucking believe it and I am still in shock behind the shit." Miracle replied.

"Wow! that's crazy." Heaven mused. It was the first time she ever heard Miracle mention her father since she known her. She use to ignore people when anyone would ask about him. Even her.

"He is suppose to be stopping by the house later so we can catch up." Miracle casually informed Heaven and wait for the volley cuss words to follow. But there was none.

"I think that would be a great thing to do Miracle. Because at the end of the day is still your father feel me? And now you will get the chance to find out why he was never around, especially after your mother passed away understand. And to be honest with you? I wish I the opportunity you have now to meet my father. But its too late because he died of aids in prison. So I think you are doing the right thing hear me?" Heaven expressed with tender emotions.

"But how do I know if he's really my father and not just some wanna be dad ass nigga?" Miracle questioned and knew deep down she was only questioning herself looking for the same answer instead of Heaven.

"Miracle, I don't think a nigga would of just came out the blue at you claiming to be your father. Where they do that at? I think he is telling the truth and the only way to find out? Is to sit and talk with the nigga feel me? Do you need me to come over there with you?" She asked at the same time Miracle heard the knock at the front door. *Oh my God! Its him.* Miracle thought and quickly said her goodbyes to Heaven and hung up.

It had felt like the longest walk of her life as she shuffled to answer the front door. *Here we go!* She thought unlocking the door and tentatively swung it open. Benjamin stood there with a nervous smile on his face as they silently stared at each other. It was an awkward moment.

"Hey baby girl." Benjamin greeted and wasn't sure if he should give her a hug or shake her hand.

"Hi." Miracle returned in small slender voice. She couldn't believe her father was standing in her doorway after so many years as she step aside and allow him into the house. Benjamin looked around impressed as he followed her into the living room and took a seat on the sofa.

"You have a beautiful home Miracle." He complimented as she sat down on the sofa across from him.

"Thank you. It wasn't easy." She confessed and her comment gave Benjamin pause as he reflected on his absence in her life and knew it must've been hard for her growing up without both parents in her life.

A pregnant silence had filled the living room and clung in the air for a long moment before Benjamin cleared his throat and started speaking.

"I know you have so many questions for me and I'm gonna try to answer everyone of them for you understand? But first, I want you to know that I never stop loving you or caring for you and wondered every second of the day how you was doing. And I loved your mother dearly. When she got pregnant with you I felt like the happiest man alive and couldn't wait for you to get here-" Benjamin had a fond look in his eyes as he reflected back on the memories.

"-There was nothing I knew I wouldn't do for you and wanted to give you every thing in this world your tiny heart desired. But I knew me and your mother couldn't afford to give you the things I imagined in my mind. So I went out there and started taking what I felt belonged to us and what I thought would make your life more easier. And things was actually going good during the beginning months of her pregnancy, until I started getting more greedier as the more money I started making. And I quickly got lost in the materialistic things of life and forgot about the real reason I started in the first place-" Miracle could see the regret etched on his face and hear the remorse in his voice as he continued speaking.

"-That was the worst mistake I could of made and it cost me everything in my life. I just didn't lose material possessions, I lost you and your mother. Right before she was due to give birth I got arrested and that's when our world fell apart. There was no amount of money that was gonna get me off the hook either. I was charged with racketeering, money laundering and two-counts of first-degree murder. It was over for me and it broke your mother. To this day, I could still hear her yelling at me *"Benny why?"* I stupidly gambled our lives and suffered a lost that has haunted me for all these years." Benjamin explained misty eyed. A couple of times he almost choked up and had to stop to gather himself together.

Miracle was lost for words as she listened to him explain the reason why he wasn't in her life for so many years and it wasn't the things he spoke that messed her head up, but it was the name he referred too, Benny! She had grew up hearing hood stories about an infamous nigga named Benny and come to find out now, the same nigga was her father? It was unbelievable. *Oh my fucking God! Wait until I tell Heaven about this shit.* She thought, looking at him with a new set of eyes.

"But enough about me for now. Tell me about yourself and what you have been doing over the years." Benjamin asked, feeling like a weight had been lifted off his shoulder. Miracle sighed and took a deep breath before she started speaking.

"I don't even know where to begin. I grew up in the foster care system and hated it so much, because the other kids use to always make fun of me. I had to fight everyday in school and learned fast how to defend myself. But I was a good student and got straight A's in school. When I got older things seemed to get worse for me. If it wasn't one thing it was another. I remember one night I walking home from my best friends house, Heaven, and some guy grabbed me at gun point and forced me into an alley where he raped me repeatedly. He beat me really bad and left me to die in the alley, but somehow my best friend found me and called the police. They never found the person who did it and everyday I use to walk around scared that he was going to find me again and kill me the next time-" Miracle's voice had a tone of sadness in it as she spoke.

"-I had felt so alone that night in the alley and even more alone when the only person that came to visit me in the hospital was my best friend. I didn't feel loved at all and it hurt knowing that no one in the world cared about me. To everyone I was just some poor black fat girl with no family-" Benjamin could feel the pain as it radiated off her words and felt the anger burning hot inside of him for not being able to protect his little girl.

"-It took years for me to begin living a normal again without being scared to walk down the street. Eventually I finished high school and found a job making decent money. I got myself a car and this place here." Miracle conceded with a smile. She was content with the way her life was now and learned a long time ago that holding onto the past wasn't healthy.

"So, how is your love life? You don't have to go into it details and I know its kind of too late for me to start acting like a father, but I do want to know if you happy." Benjamin inquired and she shook her head with a laugh. It was a genuine laugh and made Benjamin smile.

"Yes! I' am so happy with my love life. Its been the most happiest moments in life. The love of my life's name is Vincent and he is the sweetest and caring man in the world I ever met." Miracle glowed as she talk about her relationship and all the wonderful things Vincent had done for her. Benjamin was proud that she finally found happiness after all she had gone through in her life. *My daughter! She is a strong woman just like her mother.* He thought as he listened to her talk.

"I would love to met him someday he sound like a great man and I am happy for you both." Benjamin implied as the atmosphere in the living room became relaxed and comfortable. It had felt as though twenty-nine years haven't passed between them and it was a normal father and daughter night.

After many laughs and a few shared tears between them, they had decided to call it a night as Miracle walked him to the door.

"Its been so good talking to you Miracle and I hope we can do this more often if its alright with you?" Benjamin suggested he stood in the doorway of the front door.

"Yea, I would really love that...Dad." Miracle agreed with a smile on her face only a child could have for a parent.

"Me too." Benjamin confessed with fresh tears in his eyes as she called him dad. He held her tight for a long moment before giving her a tender kiss on the forehead and saying goodbye. Miracle had stood in the doorway watching him for a long time as he walked up the street until he finally disappeared out of her sight.

"I love you dad." She whispered into the night air as she turned on her heels and went back inside the house.

CHAPTER TEN

Miracle had been juggling her time between both Vincent and her Father for the past couple of weeks. They had become the two most important male figures in her life and she was enjoying every moment of it, especially the time spent with her father. Benjamin was everything she had hoped for in a father. As Miracle stood inside of the kitchen and prepped the food for tonight's up coming dinner date, Heaven had busied herself at the kitchen table doing nothing. It was her usual trademark when it came to putting something together.

"Bitch! I still can't believe Benny is your mother fucking father. That nigga was crazy as fuck. And he is still looking good as hell for real." Heaven professed with a mischievous glint her eyes and Miracle swiveled her head with her face scrunched and looked at Heaven.

"Don't even go there with your nasty ass." Miracle playfully warned with a laugh.

"Ugh! Girl bye. I wasn't saying it in that way." Heaven quipped defensively, but Miracle wasn't a fool and knew Heaven's nasty ass better than anyone, even her own damn self.

"Whatever Bitch! Can you pass me that pan from over there?" Miracle asked as she diced the hot peppers at the counter.

She had been planning a four-some dinner date with her, Vincent, Heaven and Benjamin for a week now and wanted it to go off without a hitch. Because it would be the first time everyone would be gathered together in the same room at once. It was going to be a memorable moment. Or at least she planned for it to be. Miracle was ecstatic about the past couple of months of her life and how perfect everything seemed to have turned out. A new love and another chance at having a family. A real family. She couldn't ask for anything more out of life.

"We have to start doing this kind of shit more often." Heaven suggested after she handed her the pan and went back to doing nothing.

"Bitch! You ain't doing shit but occupying space with your lazy ass. You need to be over here helping a bitch instead of sitting there scheming on my daddy's dick." Miracle chided and Heaven started laughing as she sat at the table and started rolling a blunt.

"Fuck you Bitch! And for the record? Even daddy's want to go to heaven." She shot back through laughter as she finished pearling the blunt and sparked it.

The evening had went off as planned and everyone was enjoying themselves. Miracle had put her foot in the food and it turned out delicious. Everybody had helped themselves to a second serving as they sat around the table talking and bullshitting. Miracle couldn't help but notice the way Heaven kept on stealing glances at Benjamin every time she thought nobody was paying attention. *Let me find out this bitch is smitten with my dad.* She thought, laughing to herself.

"So Vincent, my daughter has told me so many great things about you and I am happy to finally have the chance meet you in person. And to thank you for making my little girl happy." Benjamin addressed Vincent as Heaven hung onto every word that fell out his mouth as though he was talking directly to her and Miracle found it comical.

"Benny, she is my world and I love her to death. I don't know what I would do without her in my life and I want her to be in my life forever. And speaking of forever?-" Vincent paused and reached into his pocket and pulled out a small velvet box. There were loud gasps around the table as he turned and faced Miracle.

"-I am glad everyone is here to be a witness. Especially you Benny. Miracle Walters, will you be my wife?" Vincent crooned to every ones surprise as he opened the velvet box and presented a three-carat diamond ring to her. *Oh my fucking God!* Miracle thought stunned. She was totally caught off guard and had no idea Vincent was going to propose to her as she stared at the huge diamond rock.

"Yes! Hell fucking yes!" She shrieked accepting the proposal as he slipped the diamond ring onto her pudgy finger.

"Now its definitely time to turn up. A mother fucking engagement party! Congrats bitch!" Heaven shouted as everyone followed suit and raised their glasses in a toast.

The rest of the evening had flowed as smooth as the liquor and Miracle was higher than she ever been in her life and it wasn't from the booze. As the small party started to wind down into the wee hours of the morning and everybody was feeling buzzed, they had decided to call it a night before it turned into a slumber party. Miracle gave her father a hug and a kiss as she seen him to the door and Heaven wasn't too far off his heels. *Let me find out.* She thought, locking the door behind them as her and Vincent settled down for the night.

"I love so much baby." Miracle said in a voice soft with affection as she slipped out of her clothes. She never thought in a millions that she would be getting married someday.

"I love you even more beautiful and now I have the rest of my life to show you how much." Vincent promised as he drew her into his arms and kissed her passionately.

Miracle felt faint as his tongue searched out her soul and caused her cunt to throb with such intensity, that her body hummed from its vibrations. *Oh my God!* She thought with burning pleasure as it passed through her like a bolt of thunderous lust. Vincent shoved her hard onto the bed and there was a predatory look in his eyes, a ravening as he stared intently at her and crawled in-between her massive thighs.

"Ooh..Ooh..Fuck!" Miracle moaned as she felt his probing tongue invade the inside of her aching cunt.

"Ooh..Yes..Daddy!" She cried lustfully, arching her back off the bed as he snaked two-fingers inside of wetness and slowly stoked them in and out of her, while his tongue flicked relentlessly across her enlarged clit. Her swollen clit palpitated worst than a patient in cardiac arrest. Vincent pushed her thick legs high above her shoulders as he buried his face deep into the folds of her chocolate ass cheeks and gently started licking the outer rim of her asshole, before he wormed his tongue into the warm entrance of her dark tunnel. She tasted salty and tangy as he tongue fucked her asshole.

Oh my fucking God! Miracle thought as she grabbed and tugged on a shock full of her own hair as Vincent's tongue worked deep inside of her.

"Goddamn daddy...Fuck!" Miracle squealed, tossing her head from side to side. It had been an eternity since a man tossed her salad and the feel of his warm moist tongue slithering up inside of her drove her to the brink of insanity.

"Ooh..Please don't stop daddy..Ooh!" She pleaded in a throaty voice filled with lust as he worked both of her holes simultaneously with his tongue. The immense feeling was indescribable as her thick thighs shook and rumbled, as a powerful orgasm reverberated deep inside of her pussy and she exploded into a watery mess.

"Daddy fuck my ass now!" Miracle demanded. She desperately needed to feel him inside of her asshole. Vincent was much obliged as he flipped her onto her knees and positioned himself behind her. He spat a gob of saliva into the crack of her ass and used it for lubrication as he penetrated her tight hole in one swift thrust. Miracle moaned loudly and bit down on her lower lip as his thick wood stretched her tiny hole wide open.

"Ooh..Shit daddy." She cried as he slammed every inch of his manliness deep inside of her back door and started savagely pounding hard into her. The pain was searing...But felt deliciously good.

"Ugh!..Fuck Daddy." Miracle growled in a voice that sounded guttural as she clutched at the sheets and bucked in sync with his every thrust.

"Ah!..Ah!..Ooh my God daddy...Fuck me!" She panted, staring over her shoulder at Vincent with her face screwed in a mask of pleasure as the loud thunderous sound of her bare ass smacking against his flesh turned her on even more. She could feel the pressure of his pounding dick deep in her stomach. *Ooh God!...Ooh God!* Her thoughts swirled like a whirlpool inside of her head.

Miracle was lost in her own storm as the strong winds of an orgasm blew through her body and rattled her core. Her ass haven't been fucked so thoroughly good in a long time and she was enjoying every dirty second of it. She felt more filthier than a nasty whore and loved it as he rode her hard far into the morning hours.

CHAPTER ELEVEN

Heaven was beyond angry and furious. She was reeling with fury as she stared hard at Aamir with a scowl on her pretty face. The agitation reeked off her like a bomb's nuclear radiation and Aamir was afraid to approach her. She was in rare form. Aamir and Heaven had known each other for a number of years and danced together at a unisex strip club.

"Nigga! You keep coming at me for more money and more money. I told your ass the last time I wasn't giving you nothing else. You're the one who took this shit to another level not me nigga." She spat acidly in a defensive tone.

"Bitch! You knew the fucking deal we made from the start, so all that shit you talking now I ain't trying to hear it. I stuck to the end of my part and a nigga is getting tired of the fucking charades Heaven. And you still haven't handled the other part of our deal." Aamir clarified with an attitude of his own. He was fed up with playing a pawn on Heaven's chess board. His comment only infuriated Heaven more as she stood there grilling him with a hand perched on her curvaceous hip.

"Nigga! Yeah, I said I would give you some of this pussy, but your thirsty ass is making a bitch regret I even agreed to the shit. Because it's all you really give a fuck about instead of staying focused on what the fuck I asked you to do for me. But don't get a bitch wrong, your putting in a lot of work and I know the shit is getting tiresome, but you stressing me the fuck out with this nagging bullshit." Heaven expressed with a sigh of irritation.

Aamir shook his head in response to her remark as he softly laughed to himself. *This bitch is something else!* He thought as he stared at Heaven standing in the middle of the living room floor with her arms folded across her chest and her face scrunched up. She reminded him of an angry Succubus he once seen in a mythological painting, beautiful and sexy. Her attitude was turning him on.

"Listen, I ain't trying to be on some bullshit with you Heaven. But it's been a few months now since you came to me with your little game and a nigga been a star participant in the shit ever since. And I want to know when a nigga is gonna get the latter half of our deal? Is that too much for a nigga ask?" Aamir questioned with less aggression in his tone.

Heaven sucked her teeth as she listened to the desperation in his voice and was about to respond, until her rang, saving the moment.

"Hold that thought nigga!" She said to Aamir as she picked up and answered her phone.

"Hello?"

"Wassup Bitch?" It was Miracle.

"Nothing. Just in the house chilling. What about you?" Heaven asked in a short crisp voice.

"I Just got off the phone with Vincent's Mother and she wants me to go to church with her on Sunday, but I don't know. A bitch haven't been to church in years and why do it sound like you got an unexpected visit from Aunt Flow?" Miracle questioned hearing the strain in Heaven's voice.

"Shit! A bitch wish it was her period. But it's this lame ass nigga getting on my last fucking nerve for real. He's stressing a bitch out worse than cramps." Heaven fumed as she walked out of ear shot of Aamir. The nigga was notorious for ear hustling someone's conversation.

"I know it ain't the same nigga your always on the phone arguing with?" Miracle remarked with a shocked directness in her tone. Heaven was constantly beefing on the phone with the nigga every time her and Miracle hung out.

"Yea, it's his thirsty ass. But enough about that bozo. Are you gonna come chill with a bitch?" Heaven asked quickly switching the topic. Because she wasn't trying to let the nigga rent anymore space in her head. Bad enough, she was already contemplating sharing her kitty with the nigga's thirsty ass.

"Yea, I might as well. I ain't doing shit else and Vincent said he's out handling some business. So give me like a half-hour and I'll be over there." Miracle agreed and hung up.

Heaven walked backed into the living room and confronted Aamir as he sat back comfortably on the sofa with his arm out-stretched across the head rest. He looked a little too comfortable she noticed. *Oh! This nigga definitely gotta get the fuck out of here.* Heaven thought as she stood directly in front of him.

"Listen, we gonna finish talking about this some other time, because I got company about to come over and I don't think it would be best if you were here. No disrespect. So-"

"Hold the fuck up! You are rushing a nigga to leave so another nigga can slide through? Is that who you was on the phone with?" Aamir rudely interrupted her as he sprung off the sofa and stood in her face. He was so close he could of kissed her. *Oh! This nigga is tripping! He's about to get more than some pussy!* Heaven thought as she stepped back a foot in case the situation came to blows.

"First of all nigga! Back the fuck outta my face and second, it's none of your mother fucking business who I got coming to my house nigga! And just for the record nigga? It was my bitch Miracle. So yes, your ass gotta go! Bye!" Heaven spat acidly.

"Oh I see!" Aamir laughed sarcastically as he spun on his heels and headed towards the front door.

"I hope you do nigga. Now see your way out!" Heaven shot back with a mock laugh of her own as she followed him to the door and locked it behind him. *Fuck boy!* She thought as she walked back into the living room and started rolling up a blunt.

****

Miracle had arrived at Heaven's house earlier than expected and parked a few cars behind her X5 BMW as a Black Impala was pulling away from the curb. *Why is this nigga not answering his phone?* She wondered as she climbed out of the car and walked towards the front porch. She had been blowing up Vincent's phone on the drive to Heaven's house and got his voice mail every time. *Maybe he's busy.* She reasoned to herself as she knocked hard on the front door. A moment passed before the door swung open and Heaven stood in the threshold with a scowl etched on her pretty face.

"Damn bitch! I thought you was that thirsty ass nigga banging on my door again like the fucking cops. I thought you said a half hour? What the fuck you flew over here?

Come in." Heaven laughed teasingly as Miracle walked inside.

"I told your ass I wasn't doing shit and I was already dressed so I decided I might as well come right over." Miracle replied and rested her large bottom on the sofa in the living room. There was a fragrant scent of male cologne lingering in the air and it reminded her of the fragrance Vincent wore.

"Damn Hoe! You got it smelling all good up in here and thank God, because a bitch didn't want to have to smell your funky ass coochie." Miracle laughed and Heaven explicitly ran a finger along the crotch area of her tights.

"Smell this bitch! It smells cleaner than fresh picked roses and taste even better." Heaven shot back with a laugh and stuck her out stretched finger into Miracle's face.

"Ugh! Nobody want to smell that fishy shit bitch!" Miracle objected with disgust as she pushed her finger out of her face and Heaven started laughing.

"Wait until you smell this shit here bitch!-" Heaven said with a smirk, picking up the blunt off the coffee table. "-This shit is some gas and smell better than pussy!" She laughed, sparking the blunt and plopped down beside Miracle on the sofa.

The pungent smell of the weed immediately permeated the air and masked the fragrance of cologne as a thick grayish cloud of smoke filled the living room like the roof was on fire. Heaven coughed harshly as she sucked hard on the blunt and it made her throat burn as she expelled the potent smoke.

"Damn bitch! Are you alright? Don't think I'm giving your ass CPR because I'm not. A bitch don't know where your nasty ass mouth's been and it damn sure wasn't on this chocolate muffin." Miracle joked, accepting the blunt from Heaven's out stretched hand.

"Whatever hooker!-" Heaven laughed through a fit of coughs and tried to gather her bearings. "-This shit is more fire than the last sack I had for real." She added wiping at the tears pooled in her eyes. Miracle had quickly agreed, nodding her head as she suffered the same coughing spell and gagged through tear filled eyes.

"I told you it was some gas bitch. But whats good with you and the nigga Vincent? Have you seen him lately?" Heaven asked, plucking the blunt out of Miracle's hand and filled her lungs with the smoke.

"I haven't seen him since the other night at my house when we had the get together and he proposed to me. And I've been trying to reach his ass all day today, but I keep getting his fucking voice mail." Miracle complained with a slight whine in her voice. His disappearing act was driving her crazy.

"The nigga is probably busy and running around handling business. He might be getting the wedding shit together who knows." Heaven assured, placing the half finished blunt into the ashtray.

"Yea, your probably right..." miracle agreed weakly, but there was something else weighing on her mind and she wasn't sure how to express it. *Fuck it!* She concluded and continued speaking. "-Heaven, do you think he's cheating on me?" She asked with a kaleidoscope of emotions on her face.

Heaven had swiveled her head and looked at Miracle. She could see the wrinkles of worry etched on her forehead and knew the question was seriously bothering her.

"Girl! The nigga is in love with you for real and if he wasn't, then why would he even waste his time proposing to you? Especially in front of all us. Miracle you just have to go with the flow and don't let your past relationships cloud your judgment feel me? And besides, the nigga even told his own mother about the proposal. So I highly doubt the nigga's playing you." Heaven strongly affirmed as she scooped the blunt out of the ashtray and passed it to Miracle.

"Here! Lite this shit back up bitch, because your ass definitely need to smoke. So are you going to go to church with his mother on Sunday? Or you haven't decided yet?" Heaven inquired passing her the liter.

"I'm still thinking about it and haven't made my mind up because I hate going to church for real. The shit be making a bitch feel weird like the pastor is talking about me as he's quoting scriptures and it seems as though everyone in the congregation is staring at me." She confessed and Heaven started laughing shaking her head.

"Bitch! What is so damn funny?" Miracle blasted, sparking the blunt and took a leisurely toke on it.

"Your paranoid ass is funny. Ain't no pastor talking bout you bitch and mother fuckers are probably staring at you because they want to play in the sin city between your legs." Heaven teased with more laughter.

"Fuck you bitch!" Miracle retaliated in verbal barrage of profanity as she scrunched up her nose at Heaven and laughed.

"But seriously, I think you should go Miracle. It would be a good way to bond with her even more." Heaven advised as they both sat quietly engaged in their own thoughts and finished smoking the rest of the blunt.

CHAPTER TWELVE

Sunday morning had came faster than Miracle expected and she was a bundle of nerves as she paced the living room floor waiting on Mrs. Elaine to arrive. She couldn't believe she agreed to go to church with her, but it was too late to back out now because she was already on her way. *I hope the mother fucking church don't burn down, because a bitch ain't been to church in years.* Miracle thought, peeking out of the window and was about to turn away until she spotted Mrs. Elaine's car pulling up to the curb and parking. *Here I go, off to see the wizard!* She joked to herself as she gather her things and headed out of the front door.

"Hey baby, how are you doing?" Mrs. Elaine greeted as soon as Miracle climbed into the car.

"I'm doing okay. Just a little nervous." Miracle confessed, closing the door and fastening her seat belt as Mrs. Elaine pulled off into traffic. Mrs. Elaine laughed.

"Child, there's nothing to be worried about. Your going to the Lord's house. The only thing that you should be worried about? Is catching the Holy Ghost." Mrs. Elaine quipped with a reassuring smile on her face. *The Holy Ghost? Shit! that's the last thing a bitch is trying to catch. No disrespect Lord."* She thought, feeling more nervous than before just thinking about it.

Growing up, Miracle's foster parents wasn't keen on religion and only attended church services on special occasions and those occasions was rare. They rarely celebrated anything involving the lord and now looking back, Miracle had realized it was kind of strange. She didn't even recall seeing a Bible anywhere in the house. it's no wonder she felt more sinful than a brothel. But Mrs. Elaine? She was a devoted Christian, putting God above everything, even family and she never missed a church service regardless of rain, sleet or snow. Even though it hadn't always been that way for her in the past. Because in her younger days she was fast and loose, more boy crazier than a Catholic Priest. It had taken a lot of pain and heartbreak before she came crawling to the Lord.

The drive hadn't taken long as they parked in front of First Baptist Church and climbed out of the car. Miracle was taken aback at the size of the church. It was huge and reminded her of a medieval castle as she stared up at the large stone structure. She felt small and insignificant. There were small groups of people gather outside of the church as they walked up the steps towards the entrance and Mrs. Elaine greeted them before they entered inside. *Wow!* Miracle thought as she stared in wonder at the huge stained-glass window's depicting an assortment of angelic figures. It looked like a kaleidoscope of colors dancing as the sun's ray shone bright through the window's, throwing rainbows across the hard floor's surface. The wooden pew benches had a glossy shine that was polished to perfection and she couldn't believe the vastness of the church's interior as they sauntered down the aisle towards the front pew.

"Praise the lord, good to see you this morning Mrs. Elaine." An elderly woman said as they both found vacant seats and occupied them.

Miracle was astonished as she looked around at the large congregation and started feeling nervous being in the front row because she wasn't trying to be noticed by the pastor. But Mrs. Elaine was a totally different story. She looked like she wanted to draw the attention of everyone as she stood to her feet and started singing along with the choir. Miracle had wished she could vanish into thin air as she sat glued in her seat afraid to breath for the sake of catching whatever ghost possessed Mrs, Elaine.

After a litany of songs the choir finally closed with the hymn "Nothing But The Blood Of Jesus." By Andy Cherry as the pastor took to the podium.

"That is Pastor Reynolds. He delivers a mean sermon and tells it how it is." Mrs. Elaine whispered to miracle as the congregation fell under a hush and prepared to hear Pastor Reynolds preach the word. Miracle didn't respond. She was to focused on the powerful presence of Pastor Reynolds and couldn't take her eyes off of him. He looked very intimidating standing behind the pulpit and he had a saintliness that radiated off of him like a thousand watt light bulb.

"Praise the Lord! Can I get an Amen? I said can I get an Amen?" Pastor Reynolds shouted as he stared out at the congregation, like a shepherd overlooking his flock.

"Amen!" The congregation responded in unison.

Miracle had felt a surge of electrical energy sweep through the church as the thunderous voice of the congregation responded and the strange sensation caused the hairs on the back of her neck to stand up. *What the hell?* She thought as a tingling feeling coursed through-out her body. *I knew I should of stayed my ass at home!* She reeled to herself as Pastor Reynolds cleared his throat and began preaching.

"Today! I want to talk you about putting things before the Lord and I want you to listen close to what the lord has to say about that mighty sin.-" Pastor Reynolds boomed in a loud voice as his finger's swiftly turned the pages in the bible and he continued.

"-Thou shalt have no other Gods before me. It is one of the Ten Commandments. A Commandment that we break every time we open our eyes in the morning. Every time we get in our cars to go to work to get that almighty dollar. Every time we go hang-out with John, Paul or Sally.-"

There was a lot of murmuring and head nodding among the congregation as the Pastor ran off a litany of offenses against God. Miracle was caught up in the fiery sermon.

"-But the biggest sin of them all? Is gluttony! And every man, woman and child in America is guilty of it. We all want more. More money, more sex, more drugs and more food! We just can't help ourselves." Pastor Reynolds admonished and immediately, miracle started to feel uncomfortable as he mentioned food. She could of sworn he was looking directly at her when he spoke of it and she didn't dare meet his penetrating gaze, because she knew better than anyone she was guilty of the sin.

"We are living in a culture of gluttony. Overeating. Do you know that it is idolatry? Food has become an idol to so many people. You are not dealing with a hunger problem, but it's sin problem. Don't you know that your body is the temple of God?-" Pastor Reynolds paused with a dramatic flair as his beady-eyes scanned the congregation and briefly feel onto Miracle in the front pew as he wiped the sweat off of his graying brow. Instantly, she had started to sweat feeling the heat from his gaze. *Oh God!* Thought with a downcast look as he continued to preach.

"Don't you know that you yourselves are God's temple and that God's spirit dwells in your midst? If anyone destroys God temple, God will destroy that person; for God's temple is sacred, and you together are that temple.-" Pastor Reynolds recited in gruff- raspy voice as he quoted out of the book of Corinthians. "-Don't you know that life is more than food? And the body more than clothes? Our brother in Christ, Luke, admonished us about this in the scripture.-"

Miracle had started to squirm in her seat every time he mentioned the word food and felt he was talking about her, because his eyes always seemed to search her out of the crowd.

"-Gluttony is a serious sin that people take lightly. When a person is heartbroken, frustrated, grief-stricken or stressed from the daily hardships of life. Where do they turn to? Not to God to give them comfort and solace, but to a big bucket of fried chicken and biscuits.-" A small murmur of laughter arose from the congregation as Pastor Reynolds fired on. "-Food can't solve a problem God was meant to fix. Did you hear me? I said food can't solve a problem God was meant to fix. I am not saying not to eat, because it's God that provides us and sustain us with sustenance of the earth. But If you find honey, just eat enough. Too much of it will make you vomit." Pastor Reynolds boomed to a choir of Amen's.

The service had lasted more than three-hours and Miracle couldn't of have been more anxious to leave as everyone bowed their head's in closing prayer. Mrs. Elaine slipped her hand into hers as the Pastor prayed over the congregation and held it gently with a motherly affection.

"Heavenly Father, I ask in the mighty name of Jesus that you watch over and protect, each and everyone of them here today as they leave your house and go back out into a world corrupted with sin. May you give them comfort in their times of need. A comfort that only you can provide and not the comfort's of the world. In the almighty name of Jesus I pray, Amen." Pastor Reynolds finished to the unison echo's of Amen.

As they rose to leave and started filing down the aisle, Pastor Reynolds stopped them and addressed Mrs. Elaine.

"It's good to see you this morning. How is the family doing? He asked with a smile bright as an angel's halo, then turned his steely eyes on Miracle and added. "-And who might this young lady be?" He inquired. *I am the one you've been talking about all morning!* Miracle thought with a fueled rage of sarcasm. But she put on a polite smile as Mrs. Elaine introduced them.

"Pastor Reynolds I would like you to meet my Daughter-n-law to be, Miracle. She is engaged to my son Vincent." Mrs. Elaine said, proudly.

"Praise the Lord. That is such wonderful news to hear. I hope I get to officiate the wedding and speaking of Vincent, how is he doing? I haven't seen him in years." Pastor Reynolds stated, shaking Miracle hand and bidding farewell to other congregationers.

"He is doing much better nowadays. You know how he can be at times. I would love for them to have a Christian wedding, but these young people today have a different belief." Mrs. Elaine sighed with a heavy heart.

Pastor Reynolds had known Mrs. Elaine and her family since the days before he became a Pastor. He had watched Vincent grow into a man from a scrawny little boy, that couldn't seem to keep himself out of trouble.

"Make sure you tell him I hope to see him in service one of these days and I look forward to seeing you as well young lady." Pastor Reynolds said to Mrs. Elaine and smiled at Miracle as he escorted them down the aisle towards the exit doors. *Shit! it's the last time I would be here. You won't be making anymore sermon's about me!* Miracle thought to herself as she and Mrs. Elaine filed out of the church and climbed into the car.

CHAPTER THIRTEEN

Miracle had peeled out of her Sunday's best as soon as she walked into the house and tossed the sweat-stained dress into hamper. The Pastor's sermon had her sweating more than a sauna and she couldn't wait to get in the shower to cleanse his unholy words off of her body as she stripped off her undergarments. *I can't wait to tell Heaven about this bullshit!* She thought, standing under the hot-spray of the shower water. But she had to admit to herself, she really did enjoy spending the day with Mrs. Elaine. There was so much she had learned about her that she didn't know before and it endeared her even more to Mrs. Elaine. She couldn't wait to have her officially as a mother-n-law.

Once she was done showering and pampering herself, she retreated to her favorite get-away place; the kitchen. She was starving and need to replenish her spent calories, especially after sitting through the pastor's sermon. The more he had shouted and rambled on about food? The louder her stomach had growled with rebellion. *I wish his ass was here to witness the feast a bitch is about cook up!* She thought with a devilish smile on her face as she rummaged through the refrigerator. *I'll show him gluttony!* She mused, removing a large slab of bone-less ribs out of the ice-box and setting them aside to thaw out as her phone rang.

"Hello?"

"Wassup bitch! Did you catch the holy ghost at church today?" Heaven wisecracked as soon as Miracle answered the phone.

"Real funny bitch!-" Miracle laughed, placing the slab of ribs into the sink filled with warm water. "-But let me tell you about the bullshit that went down at church today! The Pastor had the mother fucking nerve to talk about gluttony in his sermon bitch and can't nobody say he wasn't talking about me, because my big ass was sitting front row and center bitch!" Miracle ranted, accusingly and heaven's high-shriek laughter could be heard on the other end of the line. She was beside herself with amusement.

"There your ass go again with that paranoid bullshit. Tell me, what made you think he was talking about you?" Heaven questioned, trying to gain composure of herself as she continued to snicker.

"Bitch! I'm serious. Every time the mother fucker mentioned anything about food? He would look directly at me." Miracle retorted, defensively. Even though a part of her knew she was being childish.

A long moment of laughter had passed before heaven was able to compose herself long enough to speak.

"Bitch! You're tripping for-real! The man was only preaching the word. You are the only person I know that go to church and think it's a conspiracy going on." Heaven laughed and Miracle couldn't help but laugh along with her. She felt like an UFO theorist.

"Whatever bitch!" Miracle shot back in response as she placed a large pan of macaroni and cheese into the oven to bake.

"Anyway, what's going on with the nigga Benny? Have you heard from him lately?" Heaven asked. But there was something in the way she asked about him. It didn't sound right and Miracle could hear it in her voice. *My Father? Why is she asking about him for? I know this bitch didn't fuck my daddy with her nasty ass!* She thought with disgust.

"He's good. I spoke to him before I left to go to church this morning. Why do you ask?" Miracle questioned.

"Oh! it's nothing.-" Heaven stated vaguely. "-I was just asking. How is Vincent doing?" She inquired.

"He's suppose to be coming over here later, so we could have Sunday dinner together. We was going to go over to his mother's house and have a family dinner, but he decided he wanted to spend time alone with only the two of us. Especially since he has been busy lately taking care of God knows what." Miracle explained, but she was still puzzling over the fact Heaven had asked about her father and she made a mental note to speak to her about later. Because right at the moment she wasn't trying to go into the matter over the phone. *It's probably nothing major anyway.* She assumed, trying to find justification for Heaven's actions as she seasoned the ribs and checked on the Macaroni inside of the oven.

Vincent had been running back and forth to lower Delaware in the past couple of days and at first, she found it very suspicious because he normally conducted his business dealings around the city. So the sudden change in his plans had her feeling some kind of way, insecure and jealous. Because she didn't have the slightest clue as to the nature of his business, but she had managed to reel in the ugly head of her insecurities.

"Oh! Shit! I almost forgot to tell you. they're having a male stripper party at the Gold Club this weekend and a bitch is definitely going to be in the building. And I think you should come too since you don't seem to have any plans with your boo!" Heaven suggested with excitement.

"Bitch! How the fuck would you know If I got any plans or not? A bitch might want to stay home and get my pussy fucked all-night long. And besides, I thought the Gold Club was shut down?" Miracle noted, removing the pan of macaroni and cheese out of the oven and coating it with another layer of cheese.

"It was closed down for awhile, but it reopened under a new management about two-months ago and I heard they remodeled the entire inside of the club. It's suppose to be the grand opening this weekend, so the shit should be popping. Do you think Vincent will let you go?" Heaven asked.

"Bitch! I am a grown ass woman and don't need nobody's permission to go anywhere! But I didn't even say if I was going or not. I have to think about it."

Miracle wasn't to keen on going to strip clubs, whether it was male or female strippers, because she didn't like the atmosphere of them and definitely couldn't stand the smell inside of the place.

"Whatever bitch! You know damn well Vincent ain't gonna let your ass go to any strip club, especially one packed with a bunch of big dicks running around!" Heaven laughed, trying to bait her into going to the club. It was the basic move of reverse psychology.

"What? We'll see. Watch a bitch be stepping out to the club looking fat-tastic!" Miracle asserted taking the bait, hook, line and sinker.

"Yay!" Heaven quipped, relishing in her art of persuasion. "We're gonna make it rain in that bitch!" She stated with a laugh and Miracle was none the wiser she had played right into her hand.

"Let me get off this phone so I could finish cooking dinner. I'll holler at you later bitch! Bye!" Miracle said, hanging up and continued putting her Sunday's dinner together as she waited on Vincent to arrive. She wasn't quit sure on how she was going to broach the subject to him about going to the club and wondered if she should even tell him about it. *Fuck it! I ain't saying shit. He don't never tell me where the fuck he be going to.* She concluded and pushed the thought out of her mind as she busied herself with setting the table for dinner.

An hour later Vincent had walked through the door and greeted her with a kiss on the forehead. He looked worn out and disheveled.

"Hey baby! Sorry I am a little late. I got held up in traffic on my way back into the city. What did you cook? It smells delicious and a nigga is starving." He asked, walking into the kitchen and sat down at the table. Miracle didn't like the look of his appearance and immediately grew suspicious, because he was usually well kept together. *I know this mother fucker ain't out there cheating on me? And I gave him a set of keys to my house? I should smell his mother fucking dick and see if the shit smell funky!* She thought as her jealously rose to the surface and her anger simmered to a broil.

"It's fine babe. I'm just glad you made it back home in one piece. I missed you!" She said, trying to pretend as if everything was okay and there wasn't nothing on her mind.

"I missed you too baby and couldn't wait to get back home to you. I had a long ass day and a nigga is tired as hell." He declared as she fixed him a plate of food.

Miracle didn't want to jump to conclusion and accuse him of cheating on her without having any solid evidence against him, besides the fact he looked a hot mess. So she kept her suspicions to herself and gave him the benefit of the doubt.

"You look tired babe. But don't worry about it my love. You know your wifey's gonna take good care of you." She said with a tantalizing smile on her face as she placed their plates on the table and sat down to eat.

"That's why I love you beautiful. So did you enjoy yourself today with my mom?" He asked, taring at a piece of rib with his fingers and shoving it into his mouth. The meat was so tender it peeled off the bone.

"Yea I had a great time with her and that Pastor of hers?..." Miracle trailed off shaking her head with a laugh. "-Lets just say he's something else." She stated and Vincent laughed.

"Yea! He could be a lot to handle. I hated going to church with my mother when I was young, because he always seemed to be talking about me when he preached." He confessed with a chuckle.

"Oh my God! I felt the same way today. I swore he was talking about me." Miracle admitted and they both started laughing at their silly suspicions.

Afterwards, Miracle had busied herself cleaning up the kitchen and putting the leftover food inside of the refrigerator as Vincent ventured off into the shower. The evening had turned out perfect and Miracle started feeling bad that she wrongfully accused him of cheating, even though she didn't voice her assumption aloud. *I have to stop being so jealous and insecure. He loves me too much and wouldn't do that to me.* She convinced herself as she finished putting everything away and headed upstairs to join Vincent in the shower.

As she ascended the stairs with her thoughts on making love to Vincent in the shower, her phone had chirped with an incoming text message and she was tempted not to open it because she was trying to get some dick. But she seen it was from her father, Benjamin and decided to read it; *"Hey, it's your dad. I really need to speak with you its important!"* Immediately she had grown concerned and her mood switched from horny to worried as she quickly dialed his number. *Oh God! I hope he' s alright.* She thought, bypassing the bathroom and heading directly into the bedroom.

"Daddy? it's me. I got your text is everything okay?" She asked as soon as he answered the phone.

"No baby girl and I am sorry. I have something to tell you." He confided, but there was a forlorn tone in his voice.

CHAPTER FOURTEEN

The past couple of days had passed by in a blur and Miracle was still suffering from the shocking news her father confided in her about. She couldn't believe what happened and didn't want to accept the truth of the situation, even though it was something she had to live with. She was stressed and wasn't in the mood to attend the grand opening of the strip club tonight, but she didn't want to renege on Heaven and decided to go ahead with their plans, thinking a room full of swinging dicks would be a better distraction than sitting alone at home dwelling on something she couldn't change. *what's taking this bitch so long to get here?* She thought, growing agitated and pulled out her phone. She wasn't beat for the games and dialed Heaven's number.

"Bitch! Where the fuck you're at?" She barked into the phone as soon as Heaven answered. She didn't even give her a chance to say hello.

"Hello to you too bitch! What do you mean where I'm at? I am about to pull up in front of your house now. I had to make a quick stop to grab some chow because you know a bitch need that fire in her and what the fuck is wrong with you? Bring your grumpy ass outside." Heaven spat and hung up.

Miracle haven't told her or anyone else about the conversation she had with her father and figured it would be best if she kept the news to herself, because it was nobody's business. It was a personal matter that she felt shouldn't be shared publicly, friend or no friend. She snatched her Veronica Ann clutch off the sofa and rushed out of the house to get in the car, before Heaven started blowing the horn like a crazed conductor.

"Bitch! I was about to start tooting this horn if your ass wasn't out here in the next minute." Heaven teased as Miracle climbed into the car and slammed the door shut with a loud thud. "-And you're gonna stop abusing my damn car before I have your ass arrested for domestic violence. Slamming my poor door like it denied you some dick." She added with a laugh as she pulled into traffic.

"Fuck you! You know a bitch is heavy handed." Miracle shot back and they both started laughing.

By the time they reached the Gold Club Miracle's mood had lightened and she started to feel more like herself as Heaven swung the X5 into the parking lot and looked for somewhere to park, but there was no parking spots available. The entire parking area was packed with a bunch of vehicles belonging to thirsty and desperate bitches vying to see some strange dick. And Heaven wasn't no exception.

"Damn! I had a feeling this shit was gonna happen and there wasn't going to be any fucking where to park. We should of got here early." heaven complained as she crossed through the intersection and parked across the road in the empty parking lot of Hak's Sports bar.

"Bitch! Are you fucking crazy? I ain't trying to be road kill because you want to cut across the fucking highway!" Miracle shrieked. Her poor chubby heart was pounding hard inside of her chest. She couldn't believe Heaven had the nerve to shoot across the highway instead of going around the bend.

US Route 13 was one of the busiest and most dangerous intersections in Wilmington, Delaware. It was known for some of the worse car accident fatalities and hit and runs in the city.

"Calm down bitch! You're still alive aren't you? So lets go with your scary ass." Heaven laughed as they both climbed out of the car and jogged across the highway towards the club.

There was a large crowd of different breeds of females outside of the Gold Club waiting to get inside and the line wrapped around the building. It looked like a dog kennel packed with a bunch of bitches in heat.

"Goddamn! You see that fucking line? It's long as a mother fucker! How the hell we're getting inside of there?" Miracle complained, staring at the throng of woman standing in line. *I ain't beat for this shit!* She thought as heaven snatched her by the hand and dragged her along towards the front entrance of the club.

"Who the fuck said anything about standing and waiting on line? I'm a boss bitch and boss bitches don't do lines. Come on!" Heaven quipped, bossing her way to the front of the line with Miracle in-tow. There were a lot of dirty looks thrown their way as they both nonchalantly strutted pass the waiting females and approached security at the front entrance.

I don't know how this bitch is suppose to get us inside of this club? She better have some pull with the security, because a bitch ain't trying to be embarrassed in front of all these people! Miracle thought, feeling apprehensive as Heaven walked boldly up to the bouncer at the door.

"Wassup J.T?" Heaven crooned in a sexy voice, addressing the bouncer at the entrance. He was a tall dark-skinned muscle bound goon with rugged features. He sort of resembled the late well-known Actor Michael Clarke Duncan from the movie; The Green Mile.

"Oh shit! Heaven whats goody? I didn't know you was going to be here?" J.T said, giving her a hug and unlatched the rope post so they could go through.

"You should've known a bitch wasn't about to miss this event. And J.T, this is my best friend, Miracle." She introduced as they stepped across the threshold of the barrier and he gave Miracle a warm-welcoming smile.

Heaven and J.T had known each other ever since they were teenagers and attended Howard High School together, but it had been a couple of years since they last seen one another.

"Hey! It's been nice seeing you again and I see your still looking good." He smiled, complimenting Heaven as her and Miracle walked inside of the club's entrance.

"How the fuck you let them bitches skip the line and go inside before us? Knowing we've been standing out this bitch for over an hour?" A heavy-set female with a bad weave complained as small bickers of complaints erupted.

"Shawty! Your raggedy ass looking lace-front weave has a better chance of getting inside than your ugly fat ass." J.T shot at the heavy-set female and a cheer of laughter erupted from those around her.

Once inside, Miracle looked around at the newly installed layout of the club and was impressed with the renovations of the place as her and Heaven made their way to the bar. There was a huge center stage with a cat walk adorned to it, along with a kaleidoscope of strobe-lights running across the top beams of the stage and there were medium-size dance cages strategically positioned around the clubs floor. It was a major upgrade from the way it looked in the past.

"This shit is packed as a mother fucker! I never would've image this many bitches came to these kind of shows." Miracle said, looking at the wall to wall body of females. It was her first time attending a male stripper event.

"It's going to be even more crowded by the end of the night. Bitches do love seeing and having dick's bouncing in their faces." Heaven quirked with a laugh, enjoying the sexually charged atmosphere as they both ordered drinks and stood about staring at the collage of scantly dressed woman.

To Miracle? The woman looked desperate and horny as they eagerly waited for the male strippers to take the stage. It was a look she could spot a mile away in the eyes of a female, because she had the same look in her eyes not so long ago. But the strangest thing that caught her attention and surprise her the most? She had noticed there were a large number of plus-size women in attendance. Not to say, there wasn't a sprinkle of petite females in the building because they were in abundance, but fewer in numbers. *Goddamn! it's a whole lot of big women in here!* She thought as the barmaid brought over their drinks and exchange for them a large amount of bills they had for singles.

"A bitch's about to make it rain in this mother fucker tonight! Heaven shouted with a laugh as they both sauntered through the throng of females and seated themselves at an empty table near the front of the stage.

The ambient sounds of the singer Ginuwine's song; Pony, had the atmosphere energized as a bevy of male strippers took to the floor, clothed with only sheaths covering their genitalia area and the horny women went wild. There were thunderous hooting and hollering as they casually approached random tables of females and started sexily gyrating in the face's of the women. Miracle couldn't believe what she was seeing and fell into a trance as a male stripper stood in front of her grinding his half-placid dick in her face. It looked long and thick covered in the sheath and she began to feel the familiar stirring between her legs as he brushed up against her. *Oh my God!* She thought with embarrassment, trying to maintain her composure. But it was something she found hard to do with a big dick bouncing in her face.

"That's right bitch! Turn the fuck up!" Heaven shouted, tossing dollar bills at the male stripper as she laughed watching the conflicted expression on Miracle's face. Heaven was enjoying her best friends sticky situation as she continued raining bills down onto the male dancer. Miracle was like a deer caught in the path of a cars headlights and wasn't sure whether she should fondle the dick or shy away from it as he steadily slow grind in front of her.

Apart of her felt as though she were cheating and caused her heart to clash with the burning lust rising inside of her, but her pussy had a mind of its own as it ached for the attention it was receiving. *Fuck it! A bitch ain't come here tonight for nothing. I might as well some fun!* She reasoned to herself and took full advantage of the dick thrust in her face as she started stuffing bills into the strippers waist band.

"Um..Make that mother fucker bounce!" Miracle cheered, cupping his tight-muscle buns and buried her face into his groin area as she unleashed the pent up freak inside of her.

"Eat that dick up bitch! Gobble it!" Heaven hollered, egging her on as another well-endowed stripper slid up beside of her and occupied her face with his dick.

Miracle was caught up in the moment and loved every minute of the attention her body was being shown as she lost herself in the raunchy lap dance. She was hot and bothered, burning with heat between her legs as sweat trickled down the temples of her face and a sticky wetness pooled inside of her panties. *Oh my fucking God! This nigga got a bitch horny as hell!* She lusted without shame, dragging her manicured nails down along his chiseled six-pack and felt the tingling of her clit throbbing between her moist thighs. She needed to be fucked, not made love too, but fucked hard and savagely.

There was women scattered through-out the club in explicit positions as male strippers erotically gyrated against their upturned asses or in-between their wide-spread legs on the floor. It looked like an orgy of writhing bodies.

"Bitch! This mother fucking club is turnt up!" Heaven beamed, exposing her perky breast and taunted them teasingly at the male stripper. *Oh my fucking God! This bitch is crazy!* Miracle thought with a shocked expression on her face as she watched him caress her hardened nibbles with his tongue. It was surreal and strangely turned her on. But the moment was short-lived as the music suddenly stopped and the DJ took to the mic.

"Listen up! We got someone entertaining for all you horny ladies out there tonight. Someone special. A real treat for your eyes and guaranteed to have you creaming in those panties if you haven't already? Ladies! Give it up for the one and only Mr. world-wide exclusive himself, Anaconda!" The DJ announced as the thunderous sounds of the rappers Nelly song; Hot in Here, boomed through the speakers and Anaconda appeared onto the stage.

The crowd of horny women had gone ballistic and a thunderous roar arose in the air, echoing through-out the club as he stepped nude into the spotlight of the stage. *What the fuck?* Miracle's mouth had dropped wide-open in shock and her pussy dried up faster than a drop of water in the desert. *Oh my fucking God! Vincent? I know A bitch ain't tripping!* She thought stunned, blindly peering through the glare of bright lights on the stage and prayed she was wrong because she didn't want to accept the truth, even though it was staring her dead in the face. But to her? The truth seemed hard to believe, until she seen the harsh reality of it written on Heaven's shocked face as she looked at her. It was Vincent!

Miracle was devastated and stuck in a state of disbelief as she watched him gyrating sexily on the stage. It had felt as though she was looking at a stranger and couldn't understand why he would hide something like this from her? There was a million questions running through her mind as a crowd of females flocked around the stage like a bunch of hungry vultures. *I can't fucking believe this shit! He's a fucking stripper? I wonder what the fuck else he has been lying to me about?* She thought as her shock turned into hurt and she shot to her feet.

"I'm leaving Heaven. I can't sit around here and watch this shit!" She said in a voice choked with tears and Heaven rose to her feet shaking her head as she stared at the scene unfolding on the stage. Women were fondling and caressing all over Vincent's naked exposed body. *So...This mother fucker has been sharing my dick with these nasty bitches?* She fumed, feeling the hurt turning into anger and was ready to cause a scene.

"Come on!" Heaven agreed. But in that same moment? Miracle's eyes had briefly locked with Vincent's and everything cease to exist.

CHAPTER FIFTEEN

Miracle was wide-awake pacing the living room floor waiting on Vincent to get home and apart of her wondered if he would even show up after their run-in at the club as her mind ran rampant with questions. *First, the bullshit going on with my father and now this?* She thought, feeling as though her once perfect world was now falling apart. it was too much for her to deal with and felt like she was going to have a nervous breakdown. Heaven had tried to assure her on the drive home that everything was going to turn out fine and he would explain the reason he was dancing at the club. But at the time she was too hurt to listen and couldn't believe he would keep a secret like that concealed from her. It was like he was living a double life and it only strengthened the belief that he was cheating on her with other women.

Now, I see why he was coming home most nights looking like a hot mess! She presumed with tears pooling in her eyes and couldn't stop them from dripping as they ran with pain down her face. *I knew this shit was too good to be true. But he want to marry me?* She thought, feeling like the past was once again repeating itself and her life was caught in the never ending cycle of rejection. It was the story of her life, chapter after chapter and she was tired of reliving the same story over and over again. *God why?...*She had started to question, until she heard the key turn in the lock on the front door and Vincent walked inside.

There was a moment of awkward silence as they both stared at one another and it felt like an eternity had passed before either on of them spoke.

"Baby! I know you're pissed off and hurt, but if you give me the chance I will explain everything to you okay?" Vincent suggested, embracing her in his arms and wiping the tears off her stained face.

"Please do Vincent." She sniffled as he led her to the sofa and they both sat down.

"Baby listen,-" Vincent sighed, taking her hand into his and looking directly into her eyes. "-I know I should've told you what I do for living when we first met, but I honestly didn't know how to tell you and thought you would take it the wrong way. I really had no intention on you finding out this way and it hurts me that you've done so understand? But Miracle dancing is all I know and I've been doing it for most of life. It's how I am able to pay my bills, buy you nice things and take you out to fancy places to eat. It's also how I am planning on paying for our wedding and honeymoon understand? It's the main reason why I am still dancing and going hard so that we won't have to ask anybody for help when the day do come. But at the same time I don't want to hurt you and will stop dancing if it bothers you because I love you too much to ever want you to feel that way." He expressed, hoping she would find it in her heart to forgive him for keeping such a secret hidden from her.

Miracle was taken aback by the honesty of his words and could hear the sincerity in his voice as he spoke, but there was still the nagging question of his faithfulness on her mind.

"Vincent, I want to ask you something and please be honest with me okay? I just want the truth that's all, no lies, no games understand? Because I already have a lot to deal with and I am not beat for any more bullshit. Are you cheating on me?" She asked, staring intensely into his eyes as her mind flashed back on the entourage of women at the club and she embraced herself for the truth. Even though it was something she wasn't ready to accept, but needed to find the answer too.

"Hell no! Baby why would you even think like that? I love you too much to ever do some foul shit like that to you. I am in love with you Miracle and only you. I am content with who I have in my life and what I want in my life baby. And all of that is you! Do you understand me? I would never cheat on you not even in secret." He stressed, putting emphases on his words as he looked her squarely back into the eyes and squeezed her hands tightly with affection.

Tears of relief had coursed down her cheeks as she wrapped her arms around his neck and kissed him passionately for a long time with every fibrous inch of her soul.

"I am so sorry babe that I over reacted and I do honestly believe you about not cheating on me. All my life babe I've been lied too, cheated on and it made it hard for me to trust people, especially in relationships. But I trust you and want this work out between us. To become your wife and to spend the rest of life loving you unconditionally. Because you are my world and the best thing that ever happened to me. I don't ever want to lose you and it scares me to even think about it." She confessed with open honesty and felt as if a burden she'd been carrying around her whole life had been lifted.

"I love you even more and don't want to lose you either. And I am sorry for not telling you the truth sooner and you don't have to worry about me keeping anything from you again okay?-" He promised, wiping the tears from her eyes. "-And what else is going on with you that I don't know about" He asked with a concerned look in his eyes.

Vincent could see by the look of uncertainty on her face that she was conflicted about telling him and he wasn't trying to push the issue because he figured she would confide in him when the time was right for her.

"Listen baby, you don't h-" He started to say, but she shushed him with a finger to his lips.

"Yes I do babe. I have to get it off my chest because it's eating me alive and I haven't told anyone else about what's going on not even my best friend, Heaven. A couple of days ago my father called me and said he had to go back to prison for catching a new drug charge. I couldn't fucking believe it when he told me and it feels like I am about to lose him again after we just found each other. I feel lost and helpless. And I have no idea what do or how to even help him." She explained with a fresh set of tears in her eyes.

"Wow! I am so sorry to hear about your father and it hurts me to see you going through this painful situation, but know that you're not alone and I am here for you understand?" He consoled, taking her back into his arms and gently rocking her as she cried on his shoulders.

****

The sounds of chirping birds could be heard singing outside of the window as the early morning dawn peeked over the horizon and she realized they must've of both fallen asleep on the sofa. *Damn! What time is it?* She thought, stretching her limbs trying to get the kinks out of her cramped body as she looked around for Vincent and figured he must be upstairs taking a shower. *I'm fucking starving and I know he gotta be too!* She thought, making a hasty bee-line towards the kitchen. But something had froze her dead in her tracks and she stopped at the threshold of the kitchen's entrance. *Hold the fuck up! Somethings not right.* She thought to herself, looking around bemused until she realized the eerie quietness of the house.

"Babe!...Babe! Are you in the shower?" She shouted, standing at the bottom landing of the stairs. There was no response.

"Vincent!" She hollered again, trying to swallow down the rising panic growing inside of her as she marched up the stairs taking them two at a time. *He gotta be in the shower and can't hear me calling him.* She reasoned to herself as she fast peddled towards the bathroom in hopes of surprising him and showering together. It was something they haven't done in awhile and there was nothing more passionate than making love in the morning under a nice warm-hot shower.

Miracle had started to get excited thinking about it and she couldn't wait to join him in the shower so he could fuck her until the water turned cold. But she'd gotten a shocking surprise as she pushed open the door and found an empty bathroom. *What the fuck?* She thought with a growing anxiety as she stormed to the bedroom and walked into the same emptiness. There was no sign of him anywhere in the house. *Don't panic bitch! I'm sure everything is good, especially after our talk last night. He probably just ran out to the store.* She counseled herself and rushed back downstairs into the living room to get her phone. As she snatched it off the coffee table and started scrolling through the contacts it came alive in her hand. Immediately she had thought it was Vincent.

"Hello? Babe?"

"Babe? I love you too bitch! But I am strictly dickly and don't bump pussies bitch! What's going on?" It was Heaven and her sunk. Now she was starting to panic.

"I don't know! I'm over here tripping the fuck out! I woke up this morning and Vincent was gone. I was just about to call him, but you called in first." Miracle explained as she headed towards the kitchen. Her stomach was starting to complain and didn't give a damn about Vincent's disappearance.

"Are you serious? What the fuck happened? Did y'all get into a fight over that club shit or something?" Heaven asked, assuming the worst because she knew niggas could be petty. But pulling a Terry McMillan(Disappearing Act) on a bitch? Was beyond being petty.

"No! We was good and that's the shit I don't understand. Why would he just up and leave like that? I don't know Heaven..." Her words trailed off and Heaven could hear the hurt in her voice as she fell into a painful silence.

"Listen M-"

"What the fuck? Hold on!" Miracle abruptly cut her off as she spied the written note tape to the refrigerator door and her heart damn near stopped from fright. *I know this nigga didn't leave a bitch a Dear John letter?* She thought, tentatively reaching for the note and pulling it off the refrigerator door. She was afraid to read it.

"Miracle! What the fuck is going on?" Heaven shouted into the phone. But there was silence on the other end of the line and she thought Miracle had hung up on her until she started speaking.

"This nigga left me a note tape the refrigerator and I swear a bitch don't want to read it, because if I do and it's some bullshit a bitch's going to flip the fuck out for real!" Miracle swore as she stared suspiciously at the note on the table like it was laced with anthrax. *I can't fucking believe this shit!* She thought in disbelief as the feeling of rejection washed over her and she felt herself beginning to sink into the murky waters of heartbreak.

"Wow! He's a petty mother fucker! If the nigga planned on leaving you? He at least could've told you to your face instead of leaving a fucking note." Heaven spat with acid dripping in her voice. But Miracle wasn't listening as she picked up the note and started reading it to herself:

Hey beautiful! Good morning. I know you probably woke up tripping and wondered where the hell I'd run off too. But I had to take care of some business and didn't want to wake you up because you looked so peaceful sleeping. And I know you're probably thinking I am out here stripping somewhere and that is far from the truth. I am actually meeting up with mother and I'm pretty sure I'm the last person she'd want a lap dance from. Lol. But I had asked her to take care of something for me and she agreed so I'm heading over there to holler at her about it. And again, I am sorry about last night and you don't have nothing to worry about. I love you baby and miss you even though its only been a couple of hours.

Love you! Vincent.

"Oh my fucking God, Heaven! I just finished reading his letter and it's not on some break up shit. I was wrong and I feel bad for even thinking some bullshit for real. He said he didn't want to wake me up and had to go see his mother about something important. Damn! A bitch was about to fall the fuck apart." Miracle admitted with an excitement of relief as she held the note pressed tightly against her chest. *Oh my God! I love this nigga so fucking much!* She thought, feeling herself slipping out of the grip of rejection and falling back into the welcoming arms of love's embrace.

"Thank God! Because you definitely had a bitch in go mode and I thought we was gonna have to bank his petty ass!" Heaven laughed, even though her words were sprinkled with some truth.

"Shut your ratchet ass up!" Miracle shot back with a laugh, then felt the nudge of her stomach and remember she had forgot to feed it.

"Did he mention what he was going over there for?" Heaven asked, but there was something peculiar in her tone.

"Nah, he just said it was something important. Something about his mother agreeing to handle to shit for him. It's probably some insurance bullshit because I know he had some issue with his car." Miracle assumed as she burglarized the refrigerator looking for something fast and easy to cook.

"The Impala?" Heaven blurted out, before she had the chance to correct herself.

"Impala?" Miracle echoed. "Bitch! Ain't nobody talking about no Impala. Are you high? Because I swear your ass need to stop smoking for real!" Miracle laughed, shaking her head as she settled on a batch of leftover fried chicken and popped it into the microwave to reheat.

"Bitch! You know what I meant and besides, I am just glad y'all are over that club bullshit because I sworn your ass was going to catch a case in there and kill one of those bitches." Heaven imparted, changing the subject quicker than a dirty bitch changed their panties.

"I was damn sure about to be on the next episode of the TV show Snapped." Miracle retorted and they both started laughing.

CHAPTER SIXTEEN

Miracle had stared up at the towering building of the court house and felt an uneasiness squirming in the pit of her stomach as she trailed alongside of her father into the building's entrance. She had been preparing herself mentally for the past couple of weeks for his court date and now that it was finally here? She wasn't ready and couldn't shake the forlorn feeling growing inside of her, because she didn't trust the court system to play fair. She had a long standing dislike for court house's ever since she was younger and hated everything about them, especially the one located in the Down-town section of Wilmington on King Street. It was more corrupt than the Bush's administration and she didn't believe in the system's so-called justice because it was only blind to its own flaws, but had perfect vision seeing the flaws of everybody else. The inner lobby of the court house was packed with a bunch of white faces in suites carrying brief cases and they were easily distinguishable among the sea of black faces in button-up shirts and jeans. It had seemed as though everybody in the hood was scheduled to appear on the same day.

Oh my fucking God! This line is too fucking long! Miracle thought, feeling agitated as she stood at the far end of the line and silently cursed the court system.

"I hope these mother fuckers re-schedule my case because I ain't trying to be sitting in this place all fucking day!" Benjamin voiced hotly, echoing the probable thoughts of every other black face in the lobby.

"Next!" An Officer of the court shouted loudly as the line started to slowly dwindle down.

Benjamin had been charged with the offense of drug-dealing and was currently out on bond awaiting trial, but his case wasn't looking good according to his attorney because of his colorful rap-sheet. He was labeled an habitual offender and faced the harsh penalty of life imprisonment, even for the smallest of offenses. It was a position most black men from the inner-city of Wilmington found themselves stuck in and there was no negotiation as far as the state of Delaware were concerned.

"About fucking time!" Miracle mumbled softly under her breath as she squeezed through the narrow passage of the metal detector and followed closely behind her father towards the east-wing elevators.

The small confines of the elevator was cramped and uncomfortable. It was packed shoulder to shoulder with offenders alongside of attorney's and the atmosphere was stuffy with tension as everyone rode in silence to the court room's located on the fourth floor of the building.

"Dad! What do you think is gonna happen today?" Miracle asked with concern in her voice as they both stepped off the elevator and found a vacant seat in the back-row of the courtroom.

"I don't know baby. But I am hoping they give me a continuation and don't try to move forward with the case today, because I really don't want to be here. It's my final plea hearing and my attorney said he would try to push for it to be rescheduled, but the Judge is a hard ass and don't be trying to grant extension. Especial in cases like mine."

He explained and she could the hear the worrisome tone in his voice as they waited for the proceedings to begin.

"Do you think they're gonna try to revoke your bond and lock you up?" She pressed, staring at the court bailiffs positioned around the room. *Please Lord, don't let them take my father back to jail.* She silently prayed and wondered if the other offenders in the court room was doing the same thing.

"Baby! To be honest? I really don't know. All I can do at this point is pray they don't and grant me another continuation so I could have more time in the free world understand?" He admitted with honesty, but Miracle didn't understand and it only strengthen the hatred she felt about the Justice system.

"All rise!" The Bailiff shouted as the Judge took to the bench and sat down.

The courtroom had fallen under a suspenseful quietness as the Judge shuffled through the case files on his desk.

"You may be seated." The Bailiff instructed. There was a collective sigh as everyone sat back down and the proceedings began. *Damn! I wish Vincent was here or at least be able to talk to him.* Miracle thought hating that she had to leave here phone in the car. It was her crutch in times of stressful situations. And right now? She needed it more than ever to hear the reassuring voice of Vincent.

Benjamin's case was the fourth one scheduled to be heard, but it appeared his attorney had it pushed to the front of the docket and it seemed as though fate was working in his favor. He guessed he wouldn't be sitting in there after all for the majority of the day as the bailiff called out his name and he approached the podium standing alongside of his attorney.

Miracle's heart had started pounding the minute she heard the bailiff call her father's name and wished she could stand at his side for extra support as she listened to the District attorney state the reasons why the court should revoke his bond.

"Your Honor, Mr. Walters is clearly a threat to society and don't have any respect in regards of the law. He has an extensive rap-sheet that proves it and he's an habitual offender with slew of felonies dating back ever since he was a Juvenile. I respectfully ask the court to revoke Mr. Walters bond pending the trial date coming up in a few days." The District Attorney proposition to the court. *What? Is he fucking crazy? Talking about revoking my father's bond?* Miracle thought in disbelief, sending another silent prayer skyward to the heavens as she sat on the edge of her seat and gripped the back post of the bench in front of her.

"Your Honor, my client, Mr. Walters doesn't present a flight risk and he isn't a threat to society despite what his past record reflects. Yes! He has had some hick-ups in the past but he has learned from his mistakes and has been abiding by the law despite the alleged charges against him. He has a daughter that is present here today your Honor-" Benjamin's attorney addressed as he turned and pointed at Miracle. "-That needs him home because he has just been reunited with her after so many years away. So I respectfully ask the court to reconsider keeping Mr. Walters out on bond pending the trial date, so he can be a father to his daughter." The Attorney pleaded to the courts.

The Judge had sat back reflectively in his chair after both sides were done stating their grounds and looked sternly at Benjamin through round-frame spectacles as he cleared his throat to speak.

"After careful consideration of both parties arguments? I find it in the best interest of the court to revoke Mr. Walter's bond due to being a flight risk and a threat to society." The Judge decided, staring pensively at Benjamin with beady-eyes as the bailiffs took position behind him. The decision he'd made caused a stir of panic to spread throughout the courtroom and other offenders started shifting nervously in their seats as the feeling of hopelessness blanketed their mind.

Miracle had shot to her feet as soon as the words left the Judge's mouth and muscled her way towards the podium but was stopped by another bailiff as her father swiveled his head and looked at her. There was a despairing look in his eyes as the bailiff place the handcuffs on his wrist and he gave her a waning smile.

"No! You can't do this to him. I need him with me. Daddy!" Miracle cried, watching as they dragged her father through the door leading to the courts holding cells.

"Please! don't do this I beg you!" She pleaded. But her pleas fell on the deaf ear's of the courts and she felt as though she was going to faint. *God, why? How could you let this happen to me huh? Why?* She questioned, blaming God for the ill-fated decision of the courts.

"I love you daddy!" She shouted at the back of Benjamin as he disappeared behind the closed door.

****

Miracle had slowly staggered out of the court building in a daze and couldn't believe she was going back home alone as she dragged her feet towards the car. Her whole

145

world had seemed to crumble in the short-span of only hours as she climbed inside of the car and rested her head on the steering wheel. *I know this can't be happening and gotta be a dream because this shit can't be real!* She imagined, feeling like she wanted to scream as she sat with her face pressed-up against the steering wheel and cried.

A lot of time had passed before she was able to gather herself together and clear her mind enough to drive as she remembered her phone was tucked away inside of the console. *I really need to talk to Vincent because I am falling apart and I don't want to be alone right now.* She conversed with herself as she rummaged through the console and retrieved her phone. As she powered it back on she had noticed the missed call from Heaven and seen she'd left a message on the voice mail. It had seemed strange because she normally don't leave any messages. *It has to be important if she went through the trouble of leaving me a voice mail.* Miracle presumed as she pressed on the button dial to listen to the message.

"You have one new message!" the automated female voice stated and replayed the recording. At first, there was nothing but a jumble of noise and she couldn't distinguish the sounds until she heard the high-pitch laughter of Heaven's voice. *This bitch must've accidentally pocket dialed me!* Miracle suspected and was about to end the recording until she caught the male voice of a man in the background. *Hold the fuck up!* She thought, listening more closely with her ear wedged tightly against the phone as she let the recording continue.

There was something vaguely familiar about the voice and she couldn't place where she heard it from because the quality of sound on the recording wasn't quite clear.

Who the fuck is she talking too? And I know I didn't just hear her tell him to take off his clothes? I know this bitch ain't about to fuck? Miracle wondered, making out only bits and pieces of the conversation as she listened. But it was enough to jog her memory about who the voice belonged too and everything went black. It was Vincent.

CHAPTER SEVENTEEN

It had taken Miracle less than ten-minutes to reach Heaven's house as she doubled parked beside a black-colored Impala and climbed out of the car. She was furious and seething with anger as she eye fucked the Impala suspiciously on her way to the front door.

Please!...Please!...Please God let it not be true! She prayed, pleading with God hoping it was all just a figment of her imagination playing tricks on her as she banged hard on the door and waited impatiently for Heaven to open it. A long moment had passed before she heard Heaven shout.

"Who the hell is banging on my door like they're fucking crazy? Aamir can you please answer the door and see who the fuck's knocking on my shit like the mother fucking police?" She heard Heaven shout from behind the closed door. *Aamir?* Miracle mused, thinking maybe she made a mistake and it wasn't Vincent's voice she heard on the recording. But it was too late to turn away now because she was already at the front door.

Then suddenly, the front door had swung open and there stood Vincent in the threshold of the doorway wearing nothing but his boxers. The moment had seemed to stand-still frozen in-time as they both stared in shock at one another and Miracle could've sworn her life flashed before her eyes. Everything she'd ever been through, the lies, shame, ridicule and the rejection's all came flooding back to her as the reality of truth awakened within her mind. *Oh God! No!* She thought as something inside of her broke and shattered into a billion unfixable pieces. It was her sanity.

The sound of Heaven's voice had snapped Miracle out of the shocked induce trance that had momentarily suspended her as she shot pass Vincent and attacked Her with a flurry of heavy-handed punches.

"Bitch! How could you do this to me huh? Tell me! Why?...Why Heaven? I thought I was your fucking sister? I loved you! Why?" Miracle ranted in rage as she landed blow after blow down on Heaven's exposed face. It had took them both, Heaven and Vincent by surprise as he tried to wrestle Miracle off her, but the damage was already done.

"Get the fuck off me nigga! I hate you and hope you fucking die! You cheating ass mother fucker! I hate your lying ass!" She barked with an acid filled tone, swinging a heavy-fist blow at his face barely missing as he grabbed her by the mid-section and held her in the tight grip of a bear hug.

"Baby!...Baby! Calm down and let me explain!" Vincent crooned, trying to coax her into relaxing but she was beyond the point of no return as Heaven laid crumbled on the living room floor in a fetus position. She was badly beaten and her pretty face was covered in blood.

"Baby?-" She scoffed, trying to squirm out of his grasp. "I ain't your mother fucking baby nigga! I fucking hate you! Get your mother fucking hands off me nigga!" She spat, slipping herself loose out of his grip and pushed him hard against the plywood wall causing the weak structure to cave-in on itself as she bolted out of the front door.

"Miracle! Miracle!" He shouted at her retreating back but she ignored his shouting screams as she climbed back into the car and sped off recklessly down the street.

"Fuck!" Vincent cursed, watching the tail-lights of her car fade away into the distance.

Miracle had drove aimlessly around the city with no destination in mind as her thoughts ran rampant through her head, replaying the vivid scene of Vincent opening the door in his boxers and seeing Heaven standing off in the background. But it was the reliving of the pain that threatened to rot away her soul as it coursed through her body like a plague and caused the suffering to be unbearable. *God! Why did you let this happen to me? Pleases Lord tell me why? What did I do to deserve this after all I've been through and suffered. How could you allow this happen?* She questioned, crying through a blurred vision of tears as the constant pain relentlessly stabbed away at her heart and she felt as though her life was coming to a sudden end.

After an endless string of turns she had found herself parked in the driveway of Vincent's mother's house and had no recollection on how she arrived there. But she figured God must've led her there for a reason since he worked in mysterious ways. It was the only thing that came to her mind and gave her a cause for being at Mrs. Elaine's house because it was the last place she wanted be. Especially after everything that had transpired between her and Vincent. *Lord! Please tell why you led me here? It's the last place I want to be right now!* She prayed, looking at the reflection of her tear stained face in the rear view mirror. Her eyes were bloodshot red and swollen with puffiness from crying. And she wasn't sure if the tears would ever stop falling.

She couldn't wrap her mind around the fact that Heaven crossed her out of all people and betrayed her knowing everything she had been through in her life as though none of it mattered. Miracle had shook her head in frustration as she sat inside of the car fuming because nothing made since anymore, not trust, loyalty or friendship and definitely not love. She was confused and deeply crushed, but what hurt her the most was the act of betrayal on Heaven's part. It was something she couldn't understand and felt it had to be more to the story because there was a lot left unexplained.

Miracle had gathered herself together so she wouldn't look like a hot mess and climbed out of the car, even though there wasn't anything she could do to change her disheveled appearance as she knocked on Mrs. Elaine's front door. It had taken a moment before Mrs. Elaine answered the door and stared in shock at the way Miracle looked, because she could see from the puffiness of her eyes that she had been crying.

And immediately, she knew something was wrong.

"Dear Lord! Are you alright child? What happened to you? Come in baby!" Mrs. Elaine said, soothingly as she step aside and let her into the house. *Your son is what happened to me!* Miracle thought, but kept her tongue in check because she wasn't the blame.

"It's a long story Mama Elaine." Miracle sighed, walking inside and taking a seat on the living room sofa.

Mrs. Elaine had gave her a comforting hug before she went into the kitchen to retrieve something to drink for them and then took a seat on the sofa next to her.

"Here baby! This will help you calm down. Now tell me what happened baby?" Mrs. Elaine said, adjusting herself and getting comfortable. Miracle sighed and took a deep breath before she spoke, even though she wasn't sure where to begin so she just came right out with it.

"Vincent cheated on me with my best friend, Heaven, and I caught them together at her house earlier." She explained and the words came pouring out of her mouth in a rush as she broke down in tears. But her words didn't surprise Mrs. Elaine because she knew it was only a matter of time before her son showed his true colors. He was just like his father. Mrs. Elaine had wrapped her arms tightly around her and held her for a long moment.

"Listen baby! That boy has always had a problem with cheating on women and I tried so many times to talk some sense into him, but he's hard headed just like his father was understand? I know it hurts baby and inside the pain feel like it's more than you can handle. But you're a strong woman Miracle and God wouldn't give you more than you can bear. No woman wants to be cheated on under any circumstances and there is no right justification for any man to do so, even Vincent. Because you don't deserve to be treated that way and right now I know your heart is broken in so many pieces, but you have to make a decision on whether or not you're going to accept it. Because no matter how much you love a man or a man say he loves you? Sometimes you can't run back to what hurt you in the first place understand me baby?" Mrs. Elaine counseled as Miracle sat sobbing uncontrollably and she understand the pain she was going through right now.

Miracle had understood everything Mrs. Elaine was telling her and knew she had a serious decision to make regarding her relationship with Vincent, but there was a part of her that didn't want to let go because she still loved him with every fiber of her soul.

"How do I give up the one thing I wanted and waited for my whole life? Ever since I was a child all I ever wanted was to be loved by someone that loves me for me and didn't care about how I looked or how fat I was understand? And when I met Vincent? He made me feel all of those things. It's the reason I can't understand why he would do this to me and with my best friend of all people." Miracle sobbed with her face buried in her hands. She was stuck at a crossroad in her life and felt that no matter which path she chose to follow it would only lead to heartache, because both roads was paved with uncertainty.

"How long have you suspected they were seeing each other?" Mrs. Elaine asked, rubbing on her back soothingly as the pain racked her body and she trembled with sobs.

"Mama Elaine, I don't really know and I had wondered the same thing myself. But the thing that confuses me the most? Is that she called him Aamir and I never heard him refer to himself by that name. So I don't have the slightest clue as to how long they've been messing around on me. I only just recently found out the truth about him being a male stripper." Miracle expressed, trying to still the sobs racking her body. But it was a losing effort and the tears kept flowing like a broken spigot down her face.

"Aamir is the name he been going by for some years now. He had changed his name when he turned Muslim a few years back and it's the reason I told the pastor we wouldn't be having a Christian wedding because I knew Vincent would be oppose to it." Mrs. Elaine informed her and the news shocked Miracle because now she was starting to see the picture more clearly as her mind flashed back on the day at church. But she still couldn't see the whole picture. *Why he never told me he was Muslim and that his name was Aamir?* She wondered, feeling the fangs of deception sinking deeper into the neck of her soul.

"I can't believe he never told me this? And neither did Heaven for that matter and she'd known about this the whole entire time. The part I don't understand and I am confused about is why would they keep it secret from me in the first place?" Miracle questioned, even though it was stated more than a question. Her mind was spinning with suspicion as she sat there conversing with Mrs. Elaine through-out the evening and she didn't finally leave until the wee-hours of the morning.

CHAPTER EIGHTEEN

Miracle had become reclusive in the past following weeks and took to becoming a hermit inside of the house because she didn't want to be bothered and wanted to be left alone as she sulked in the loneliness that surrounded her. As it once again became the better half of her existence. There was no more romance in paradise for her and being outside seeing other happy couples only reminded her of the lost in her life. So she had shunned the outside world and didn't want to have anything to do with anybody. She had even quit her job without notice, despite having a mountain of bills piling up because she couldn't stomach the thought of being cramped in a small office around people she cared nothing about and that doubled for the skinny bitch, Kimberly.

She was stuck in a state of severe depression that had grown deeper with each passing day and she couldn't find a way of escaping the pain that encompassed her soul leaving her suffering in misery. It was to the point even her home life suffered in the aftermath of the pain. She was living in a pigsty of filth and gave up doing the mundane task of cleaning her once tidy house. There were empty food containers scattered around the floor and dirty dishes littered the coffee table in the living room. She even neglected to bathe herself and couldn't remember the last time she had taken a shower. It was a lonely hell of heartache. The only source of comfort she had came from the food she consumed, non-stop, as she over-indulged herself trying to eat away the pain. But the pain was ever present and constant, stubbornly refusing to give her a reprieve of the torment it lashed out no matter how much food she ate.

Miracle was faded after smoking a blunt to the face. She was stuck in her own zone as she laid sprawled on the sofa listening to the song; Unbreak my Heart and topping off her fourth tub of ice cream when her phone had rang, interrupting her Toni Braxton moment. It was the umpteenth time it had rang and she ignored every last call, even though she was tempted at times to answer it. But she couldn't find the strength in herself to pick up and face Heaven, even though she knew the conversation had to eventually happened at some point. But right now wasn't the time. *I wish this bitch stop blowing up my fucking phone. Can't she see a bitch ain't trying to talk or be bother?* She thought aggravated as she tossed the empty ice cream container amongst the rest of the filth and went to get another one.

There was a part of her that still loved Heaven and she missed her so much, despite everything that had happened between them. They were best friend and nothing could ever change the love she had in her heart for her. But in truth? The emotional pain was still too raw for her to accept and the act of betrayal was too fresh in her mind. And talking to her would only reopen the festering wound that was still oozing with grief. It had been a game of phone tag between Heaven and Vincent as they both tried reaching out to call her, but it was Heaven that blew her phone up the most. Vincent had seemed to have care and left messages on her voice mail professing his love for her, but his words seemed shallow as an unmarked grave to her. Spoken only out of pity instead of genuine affection.

Miracle had scrunched up her face as she caught a whiff of the funk emitting off her body and shrugged to herself as she sat back down on the sofa with her new rebound love, Haagen-Dazs. She couldn't keep her hands off the tasty ice cream. It was the only company she found any solace in being around. *I guess it's just me and you my love.* She mused to herself, talking to the pint of ice cream as she scooped a hefty mouthful into her mouth. But before she had a chance to savor its taste there was a knock at the front door and she paused in mid-swallow wondering who could it be banging on her door, until she heard the unmistakable voice of Heaven calling her name. *I know this bitch didn't just show up at my fucking house?* She thought surprised at Heaven's boldness and ignored the knocking as she continued to eat her ice cream.

"Miracle! I know you're in there and you hear me knocking on the door. I really need to talk with you it's important and I am so sorry about what happened between us, but you need to hear what I have to say. Please! Open the door." Heaven shouted through the closed door.

Heaven's incessant pleading had eventually softened her resolve and she finally opened the door, even though it had taken everything inside of her to do so.

"What?...What the fuck do you want now? You already took everything that meant something to me! So what is it that you could possibly have to say to me?" Miracle spat acidly, swinging open the door and stood blocking the threshold so Heaven couldn't just walk inside of the house. Heaven had remained quiet for a brief moment and accepted the verbal abuse Miracle flung her way before she started speaking.

"I know I am the last person you want to see right now, but there is a lot of things I need to explained to you, Miracle, like the truth and how all this shit happened in the first place. So can I please come in and talk to you?" Heaven begged with sincerity in her words as she stood in the doorway.

The telltale marks of bruising were still evident on Heaven's face and Miracle couldn't help but notice them as she finally relented and allowed her into the house. The pungent order of stale funk and spoiled food immediately assaulted Heaven's nose as soon she stepped into the living room. *What the fuck? Oh my fucking God!* She thought, taken aback at the smell and the filth scattered around the living room. She couldn't believe how far Miracle had let herself go and she felt bad knowing she was partially the blame. She had no idea about how much her actions had affected her and never wanted to see her in the type of condition she was in now. It had touched a deep part in her soul as she found an uncluttered spot on the sofa and sat down. But at the same time, she knew telling her the truth was going to devastate her even more.

"So... what is it that's so important you have to tell me?" Miracle asked, getting straight to the point and wasted no time beating around the bush with idle chit-chat.

Heaven had taken a deep breath and looked hard at her for a long time before she finally responded.

"Miracle, I know what I am about to say to you is going to hurt you, but you need to know the truth regardless of how much it does. And it's something I should of told you from the beginning, but I thought it would be better if I just let it flow and keep it to myself. Now I can see I was so wrong for doing it…" Heaven had paused for a brief second to gather her thoughts and Miracle sighed with impatience, wishing she would say whatever it was she came there to talk about.

"-I have known Aamir…Well Vincent for a long time now. I had met him when I use to be stripping back in the days an-"

"Hold the fuck up! What do you mean back in the days when you was stripping? I never knew you was a stripper and when the fuck was this?" Miracle interrupted, looking at her questionably and wondered what other secrets she was hiding from her.

"I started stripping after we left the foster home. It was how I was able to afford to buy us all those clothes and get that apartment I had over on Pine Street remember?" Heaven admitted, reminding her of the one-bedroom shack she had on the East side of the city. But Miracle didn't need no reminders about the apartment because she practically lived there with her. But it was the stripping part she had no knowledge about and was curious to find out about.

"I remember the apartment yea. But what I don't remember anything about? Is you being a fucking stripper! I thought you was working at mother fucking ShopRite? So what the fuck you lied to me?" Miracle accused. Her eyes blazed with suspicion as she stared steely at Heaven.

"I wasn't lying to you to hurt you or trying to be spiteful. I just didn't want you worrying about me travel to different places dancing understand? Even though I know I should of told you because we shared everything together and wasn't suppose to keep secrets from one another.

And I am sorry." Heaven expressed with a downcast look on her face. Miracle had scoffed with a laugh.

"Yea you're right! We was suppose to share everything...Except sharing the same nigga! But I guess you had to have you cake and eat it right? But lets get back to what the fuck you came here to tell me shall we!" Miracle suggested, feeling as though she was meeting the real Heaven for the first time. *I can't believe this bitch had been stripping the whole time! She was probably selling her funky ass pussy too!* She thought to herself as Heaven continued to speak.

"Well, that is when I first met Vincent and we became kind of tight because we were dancing at the same club. An-"

"So let me guess? You fucked the nigga then too?" Miracle interjected with sarcasm as she beamed daggers of disgust at her with eyes. She couldn't believe she had the audacity to be bragging about the shit in her face. *Oh! This bitch is asking to get her ass whipped again!* She thought and was two-seconds away from smacking the shit out of Heaven...Again.

"Miracle! It wasn't nothing like that! Can you please just let me finish? Anyway, we got cool as fuck and hung-out a few times but that was it. There wasn't any fucking going on between us, even though he did try to holla at me a couple times but I had shut him down." Heaven explained with honesty and hope she believed her. But Miracle was as skeptic as a non-believer in Jesus as she gave her a look of disbelief. *Yea right bitch!* She thought, but kept her thoughts to herself at the moment.

"Then why was you so quick to fuck the nigga now? Because I had him and I was finally happy to find a nigga I thought loved me?" Miracle questioned hotly as she felt the anger boiling inside of her and wanted to reach-out and choke the shit out of her. But she didn't do it and it had taken every ounce of strength inside of her not to do so.

"It was nothing like that Miracle and you have to believe me. I love you like a sister and wouldn't do anything to intentionally hurt you understand? I fucked up Miracle and the shit hurts me every mother fucking day knowing I hurt you. The shit wasn't suppose to happen like this! I swear on God!" Heaven choked as her eyes started flooding with tears. But they were tears Miracle didn't give a fuck about, because she haven't stopped crying since the shit happened to her and nobody seem to give a fuck about the way she felt.

"What wasn't suppose to happen Heaven tell me?" Miracle stressed, feeling a foreboding rising in the pit of her stomach. *This bitch better spit out whatever the fuck it is she's talking about before I strangle her ass!* She brooded as she readied herself for whatever was about to fall-out of her mouth.

"You being hurt Miracle wasn't suppose to happen. A couple of weeks before we went to the club I was feeling bad for you after that other nigga played you and you was feeling like nobody wanted to mess with you. So, I had a talk with Vincent about the situation and wondered if he had a friend I could hook you up with. But he said he didn't and I was wondering what I could do as your sister to get you out of the depressed state you was in. And at first, I was gonna just try to take you to mall or somewhere to show you a good time, but I knew that wouldn't work because you was really stressed the fuck out..." Heaven had to pause for a minute to catch her breath because she was talking too fast and then continued.

"-So, I came up with the idea of Vincent talking to you and taking you out. But I didn't want to introduce y'all and I figured it would come off better if he approached you on his own at the club the night went there. But at first he wasn't trying to do it no matter how much I begged him, until I told him I would pay him and then he agreed to do it but he added an additional cost with it. He said I had to give him some pussy as well." Heaven explained and looked at Miracle with deep regret in her eyes.

Miracle was totally caught off guard by the words that came out of her mouth and they hit her harder than anything that she ever felt in her life, even losing her father for the second time as something inside of her detonated and exploded on contact like a nuclear missile hitting the White House. The felt worse than the act of treason.

"Bitch! You mean to tell me...All this fucking time it all been a fucking lie? A hoax? A mother fucking deal you made?-" Miracle exploded like the fire works at a Fourth of July day parade as she shoot to her feet and came within inches of Heaven's face.

"-Bitch! Are you crazy huh? How the fuck could you do some shit like that to me? But you love me like a sister? Do you know how fucking happy I was and thought I had finally found a nigga that loved me for me? I was head over fucking heels in love with him Heaven! Deeply in fucking love and now only to find out you both plan this shit together? How the fuck do you think feel huh? Tell me bitch! You think because you told me the truth it's suppose to make a bitch feel better? Or set me free? New flash bitch, this ain't no fucking gospel!" Miracle ranted with rage poking her finger into Heaven's face and silently dared her to jump bad as she stood menacingly over her.

But Heaven wasn't that crazy and remained seated on the sofa because she wasn't trying to fight Miracle.

"Miracle listen to m-" she started to say, but Miracle had quickly shut her down.

"No bitch! You mother fucking listen to me! I fucking hate you and don't ever want to see your fucking face again. Lose my fucking number and act like we never met bitch! I will never forgive and I will forget you ever existed because you hurt me more than anybody ever did in my life. Now get the fuck out of my house before I kill you! And I mean every word bitch!" Miracle threatened with an underlining warning in her words and Heaven read it as she quickly rose to her feet to leave.

"Oh! And before you leave bitch take this shit with you!" Miracle added, tugging the engagement ring off her finger and chucking it at Heaven.

CHAPTER NINETEEN

"Arrgh!" Miracle screamed, feeling the agonizing pain rip through her body sharper than a bladed knife as she grabbed anything and everything within her reach and began throwing it at the wall in the living room. There was a resounding crash as vase lamp smashed against the wall shattering into a million pieces of shard glass. The lamp was a house warming gift she had gotten from Heaven and now it was shattered in pieces along with their friendship.

"I hate my fucking life!... Arrgh!" She shouted at the walls stained with food splatter and indentations as she continued to storm through the house raging like a tornado and leaving a mess of destruction in her wake. It was beyond disaster. The inside of her house resembled the aftermath of Hurricane Katrina. *Why God?...Why?...Please!...Tell me why?* She bemoaned, slumping down heavily against the wall with her knee's pressed in close to her chest and shook with violent sobs as she cried into her the palms of her hands.

She couldn't believe the words Heaven had echoed before she left and they flashed bright as a burning flare in her mind as she thought back on the signs she should've seen in the beginning. But she had been so blinded by the desperate need of wanting to be loved and to feel the affections of a man that she lost sight of the true nature of love. Because it wasn't a coincidence that love happened to find her in the club that night, but an ill-fated trick that was played on her by Heaven and Vincent. She had thought about the times she heard them both talking on the phone and couldn't believe she didn't connected the dots then, because her mind was to busy wrapped around the illusion of finding a man that loved her. *I must've been stupid as fuck to believe I had found the love I always searched for my whole life!* She thought, grabbing a shock of her hair and pulling on it in frustration as she shook her head yowling up at the ceiling. She was beginning to spiral out of control.

After a long spell of hibernating on the floor curled up in a ball of pain, Miracle had started feeling sick to her stomach and felt like she was about to puke up everything her hungry mouth had gobbled down as she rose off the floor to grab her phone. But she had swallowed down the vile tasting bile inside of her mouth and dialed Vincent's number. Her stomach had been feeling strange for the past couple of days and figured it had came from the amount of food she's been greedily consuming everyday. So she had completely ignored the persistent ache of her stomach.

"Hello, Vincent? Or should I say Aamir?" Miracle spat with sarcasm into the phone as soon as she heard his voice.

"We need to talk nigga!" She stated in a stern but firm manner, kicking around liter as she paced about the living room floor with a despondent look in her eyes.

"I have been trying to reach you for awhile now miracle so we could talk and I am so happy that you called me back finally because I've been worried about you." He crooned in a baritone voice and she laughed, but it was a laugh laced with sarcasm and amusement. *Worried about me? Really nigga?* She thought to herself and couldn't believe he had the audacity to say he was worried about her.

"Listen, Vincent! Save that worried shit for the next bitch's heart you decide to run game on nigga! Because I ain't beat for no more lies understand? The reason I am calling is because I had a little heart to heart chat with Heaven and she told me everything... And I mean everything nigga!..." She intoned and paused in a dramatic flair to allow her words to fully sink in before she continued.

"So I am going to ask you something and you better not try to lie to me nigga, because I already know the truth. I just need to hear you say the shit out of your own fucking mouth. Did you ever really love me?" She asked in a deliberately low tone that sounded more like a menacing whisper. Vincent had gone quiet and didn't respond for a very long period of time. *I know this mother fucking nigga heard me!* She thought, feeling the anger beginning to rage anew inside of her, until he began to finally speak.

"At first, in the beginning I didn't love you Miracle and it was just a game to me. So I could get some extra paper and get the chance to sleep with Heaven in the process feel me? But as time went by and I truly got to know you as a person? I started to really care about you and I began to fall hard for you. And then, it was no longer a game to a nigga because I started having real feelings for you. There were some many times I wanted to tell you the truth and came so close to telling you, but a nigga didn't know how to come out and say it to you. So I left the situation alone and let it happen however it was going to happen feel me?" He admitted, but his words had sounded trite to Miracle and she didn't believe nothing that came out of his mouth, because nigga's always said the same bullshit.

"Nigga! You're lying! Stop fucking lying to me! You never fucking loved me Vincent and even your own fucking mother said you was a no good nigga! Just like your fucking daddy nigga! So miss me with the bullshit nigga and keep it a fucking hundred with me! You never loved me then and you don't love me the fuck now!" She accused, barking loudly into the phone and spewed spittle as she screamed. The sound of her loud voice echoed and bounced off the living room walls. She was hotter than a race engine and wished it was his neck held tightly in her grasp instead of the phone.

"Miracle, I am not lying to you. I am telling you the truth. Did I fuck up? Yes, I did fuck up by lying and playing games in the beginning, but I really do have feelings for you and want to be with you an-"

"Be with me nigga? Really? If you wanted to really be with me Vincent then you would of never fucked Heaven nigga! Regardless of whatever fucking deal y'all had between the both of you. So again nigga miss me with the bullshit! You fooled me once and your cheating ass may have fooled me twice. But the next trick is on your lying ass nigga!" Miracle shot, sharply cutting him off like an amputee's leg sliced at the knee. The more he talked and the more lies that came out of his mouth? The more angrier she had started to feel. It was to the point she had tears of seething rage pouring out of her eyes and all she wanted to do was die, and take everybody with her.

"Miracle, listen to me please! I am being a hundred with you and I know its hard for you to believe after a nigga done, but it's true I do love you Miracle. And I am sorry I hurt you and I wish I could take it back but I can't understand? But at least give a nigga a chance to make the shit right between us feel me? I love you!" Vincent stressed, emptying out his heart to her and he was professing the truth, but after so many lies his words sounded like a honeycomb bear trap to her ears. Sweet, and laced with deadly poison.

"So...Let me guess! You loved me so fucking much? It was the reason you proposed to me right? Wanted me to be your wife right? And live happily ever after, right? No mother fucker! It was all just a big fucking front, a show, that you and that bitch put on! But what hurt the most nigga? Is you fucking lied to me and lied to my father in front of our faces. I will never forgive you nigga and I will never forget what the fuck you done to me Vincent! You lifted me up so fucking high only to let go and drop me like I wasn't shit nigga! Before I met you? I hated myself so much and how I looked. It was to the point I couldn't stand to look at myself in the fucking mirror. But you had changed that and made me feel good about myself, worthy, and deserving of love. Only to fucking find out it was all nothing but a fucking game and lies. I hate you nigga! I hate you...I hate you...I fucking hate you!" Miracle ranted and chucked her phone hard against the living room wall, shattering it into pieces.

It was the moment everything had forever changed inside of her and she no longer cared about anything in life, even her own, as she screamed at the top of her lungs until she felt faint and came close to passing out.

CHAPTER TWENTY

Mrs. Elaine had been worried sick about Miracle and haven't heard from her since the day she popped up at the house looking distraught, after the incident had taken place between her and Vincent. It had felt sort of strange that she haven't spoken to her in awhile, because they usually talked on a regular basis to one another. So it struck her as being very odd that she wasn't answering her phone and it was going straight to voice mail. *Lord, I hope that poor child is alright? Because I know first hand the pain she's in and what she is going through!* She thought, shaking her head worried as she waited on Vincent to return from using the bathroom. It was time they had a long overdue discussion.

"Have a seat Vincent. We really need to talk and have a heart to heart discussion about the way you treated that poor girl, Miracle." Mrs. Elaine informed him as soon he entered the living room and immediately, his face had frowned up because he wasn't trying to hear it.

"Boy! You better fix your damn face and sit your narrow ass down before I get off this couch!" She scolded, pointing a threatening finger at him and he knew her words wasn't an idle threat as he quickly parked his rear on the sofa.

"Ma! Please! I am really not in the mood to talk about the situation that had happened between me and her." He stated with a whine in his voice.

"Boy! I don't give a damn what you're in the mood for understand me? Because what you've done to that poor girl wasn't right! And you should of known better to do something like that Vincent. But what I can't figure out for the death of me? Is why you didn't tell that girl you didn't love her instead of playing with her feelings?" She asked as he sat across from her with a pout stenciled on his face.

Vincent had sighed and shook his head with downcast eyes as he sat quietly for a moment before he spoke.

"Ma, You are absolutely right! I should've of been honest with her from the beginning and told her the truth about what was going on, but I couldn't bring myself to admit it to her. Maybe I didn't feel man enough at the time, I don't know? And I'm not trying to justify my actions because I know I was wrong at the end of the day. But what I do know now? Is that I love her and want to be with her and have her as my wife." He professed with tears pooling in his eyes and she believed him.

Mrs. Elaine had never seen her son cry before over a woman and instinctively knew as a mother he wasn't lying to her.

"Vincent, have you tried to reach out to her and tell her everything you're sitting here telling me? Because she is the one that needs to hear those words out of your mouth, so she could stop hurting and find peace within herself understand me? She is grieving right now because no woman wants to feel unloved or get cheated on by the one man they believe truly love them. So you must make amends Vincent and fix the situation before it becomes unmendable understand? When was the last time you've spoken to her?" She asked.

"I've actually spoken to her the other day and she wasn't trying to hear anything I had to say to her. Because she didn't believe me when I told her I loved her and I honestly don't know what else to do about the situation." He confessed without shame.

Vincent had grown to love Miracle once he really took the time to know her and realized the true beauty inside of her, despite however the way she might've appeared on the outside. She was caring, affectionate, lovable and loyal to a fault. She had a bright personality and he loved how she made him laugh. He had never found any of those kind of qualities she possessed in any other woman he ever dated before and knew deep within himself that he had to get her back somehow or some kind of way.

"I've tried calling her myself yesterday and today, but her phone's been going straight to the voice mail. Maybe she doesn't want to be bothered baby? Because she is still going through the pain of you cheating on her and lying to her. So just give the girl sometime and leave it in the Lord's hands. And she'll eventually start feeling better." She said with a reassuring smile on her face as she rose off the sofa and gave him an affectionate hug.

"Oh! And one more thing! If I was you? I would stop messing around with that other girl. You hear me?" She advised in a motherly fashion.

"I already did the other day when I picked up the ring from her and gave her the key Miracle had let me borrow." He replied over his shoulder as he left out of the house and climbed into the car.

****

Heaven had been stationary outside of Miracle's house for a long time as she sat inside of the car and wondered if it was a good idea showing up unannounced and uninvited, because their last conversation didn't end on a pleasant note. But she was worried about her and wanted to make sure everything was fine with her, despite the fallout that had taken place between them. Because to her? She was still her best friend and sister, even though their friendship was strained at the moment. *Please! Answer the phone Miracle Whip!* She silently prayed. It was a nickname she haven't called her since childhood and it brought back fond memories of their past as a small smile appeared at the corner's of her mouth. *I love you and miss you so much bestie-sister.* She thought as she sat in the sweltering heat of the car sweating and hoped she answered the phone, but it had gone straight to voice mail again.

Fuck this! She resigned, climbing out of the car and walked briskly across the street to the house. *She's just gonna have to cuss a bitch the fuck out!... fuck it!* She thought determined as she bang on the front door and waited. A long moment had passed without any response, so she banged harder on the door and figured she couldn't hear the knocking because she was either sleeping or using the bathroom. But there was still no response. Frustrated, she was tempted to use the key she had gotten back from Vincent the other day and use it to let herself into the house as she banged more loudly on the door again. *I know she can't be sleeping that mother fucking hard and don't hear me banging on the door!* She thought, knowing for a fact she was home because her car was parked in front of the house and she never traveled anywhere without driving. *I know she ain't being this fucking petty and ignoring me by not answering the door?* She thought, removing the key out of her pocket and stuck it into the lock on the door.

"Miracle! Its me, Heaven!" She tentatively called-out as she crossed the threshold of the doorway and gently closed the door behind her.

The house was covered in a blanket of quietness as she ventured further into the living room looking for any sign of Miracle and was taken aback by the remarkable cleanliness of the place, because it was a far cry away from how it looked the last time she was there. Everything was spotless and neat. *She has to be upstairs sleeping!* She reasoned to herself, after realizing she wasn't nowhere downstairs and ascended the steps heading upstairs toward the bedroom.

There was an unearthly silence in the hallway and she felt spooked by the rising feeling of foreboding that had came over her as she pushed open the bedroom door. *I hope she's in here!* She thought to herself and then smiled, as she seen her prone form curled up in the bed. She was fast asleep with the sheet tucked firmly under her neck.

"Miracle! Get up it's me, Heaven." She said in a loud whispering voice, because she didn't want to startle her awake and scare her half to death. But she didn't budge an inch.

"Miracle! get up!" she said again in a more louder voice as she approached the bed and shook her by the shoulder. *This bitch sleep harder than a bear in hibernation!* She thought, shaking her head and shook her by the shoulder's even harder.

"Miracle! Miracle!" She shouted with no regards to frightening her as the earlier feeling of foreboding came washing back over her. Something was definitely not right. In a self-induced state of panic she had checked to see if she wasn't breathing and sighed with relief as she noticed the steady rise and fall of her stomach.

"Miracle! Wake the fuck u-" Heaven had began to shout until she noticed an empty bottle of sleeping pills laying on the nightstand table.

Oh my fucking God! No! She thought, stricken with panic as the worse fear she could've imagined turned into reality and she quickly reached for her phone to call the ambulance. Her heart was pounding hard inside of her chest and she hoped it wasn't too late.

Please!...Please!...Please! Be alright Miracle!...Please! Just get keep on breathing! She silently prayed as she waited for the line to be picked up by emergency personnel.

"Nine-one-one, what's your emergency?" The voice of a female operator implored.

"Yes! I need an ambulance please hurry! My sister had taken a whole bottle of sleeping pills and I can't wake her up ca-"

"Ma'am! Ma'am! Please try to calm down. What is your name Ma'am and your address?" The operator asked, cutting her off with a litany of questions.

"I am fucking calm! I need you to send a fucking ambulance now! I am at twelve-forty-two Jessup Street! Please hurry!" Heaven barked, hanging up the phone before the operator had a chance to question her any further and focused her attention back on Miracle.

"Please! Please! Stay with me Miracle and keep on breathing! Everything is going to be alright and the ambulance is on its way." Heaven sobbed, gently stroking Miracle's hair and prayed the ambulance wouldn't take forever to arrive as it normally tends to do when it comes to someone from the hood.

Miracle's breathing had began to get shallow, each breath becoming shorter than the last one and Heaven grew more worried because she was emitting a raspy sound every time she inhaled. *Please! Lord don't let her die! Please!* Heaven prayed, feeling a sense of hopelessness because there was nothing she could do to help her as the sounds of siren's could be heard in the distance.

****

The emergency room at the Saint Francis Hospital was crowed and bustling with activity as Heaven paced around nervously in the waiting area praying that Miracle would survive the ordeal, because on the ambulance ride to the hospital the paramedics almost lost her. It was a terrifying experience for Heaven as she watched them work frantically to keep her best friend alive and the image of it would be stuck in her mind forever. She had never prayed more harder in her life as she done at that moment and it was something she never wanted to witness again.

Heaven wasn't allowed to be at Miracle's side as they carted her off into the back towards the operating room and was pissed at the doctor's because she couldn't be present in the room during the procedure. *God! Please look after my friend and don't let her die! It's is all my fault Lord. Oh God!... I never should have tried to hook her up with anybody and lied to her. I am so sorry Lord! Please don't let her die because I wasn't the sister I should have been to her.* She fervently prayed with tears streaming down her face, hoping God would grant her forgiveness and spare Miracle's life as she paced the tile off the floor in the waiting room area. But the truth was a hard pill to swallow and she felt guilty knowing she was the reason behind her best friend being placed in the hospital.

Somebody better fucking tell me what the fuck is going on! Heaven thought with frustration as she stormed out of the waiting and approached the nurse's station. She wasn't beat for the games. It was one of the reason she couldn't stand Saint Francis Hospital because they always gave people the runaround, talking about that policy bullshit.

"Um..Excuse! Can you please tell me what's going on with my sister? She was just brought in here for over dosing on sleeping pills." She asked politely, trying to keep her temper under control. But the nurse didn't respond and had kept her face glued to the screen of the computer in front of her. The nurse was a short and roundish looking woman with a pudgy red face. *I know this fat-bitch fucking heard me!* Heaven fumed. She was ready to explode off a volley of cuss words at the nurse and it took a lot of restraint to keep her tongue in check, because she didn't want to kicked out by the hospital's security.

"Um..Excuse me!-" She repeated a bit more loudly. "-Can somebody please tell me what the hell's going on with my sister?" Heaven stated assertively. She was starting to lose her composure fast.

"Yes! May help you?" The nurse asked, looking up from the monitor screen. *Yea! Bitch! Why else would I be fucking standing here?* Heaven wanted to say but kept her thought's tightly bottled up.

"Yes! I am trying to find out what's going on with my sister? Her name is Miracle Walters and she was just brought in a little ago." Heaven replied and waited as the nurse returned her attention back to the computer. A long moment had passed before the nurse finally looked back up at Heaven and spoke.

"You said Miracle Walters right?...Yes, I have her in the system and she is still being treated in operating room. There will be someone coming out shortly to talk to you Ma'am. Please be patient and try not worry because everything will be fine. She's in good care Ma'am." The nurse assured, returning her focus back to the computer screen and left Heaven with more questions than answers as she slowly made her way back to the waiting area.

Shortly had turned into hours as Heaven's legs grew tired from the constant pacing and her patience wore thin because no one still haven't shown up to speak with her about Miracle's condition. *What the fuck is taking these mother fuckers so long? I swear these fucking people are something else!* She thought, looking around at the other face's in the waiting room and wondered if they was feeling the same way. Lost and in the dark. It was the not knowing part that was killing her. *Oh shit! How the fuck did I forget?* She thought, shaking her head, after realizing she had forgotten to call Vincent about the situation that happened as she pulled out her phone and dialed his number.

"Vincent! It's Heaven. You have to get to the hospital right now! It's about Miracle! She had taken a whole bottle of sleeping pills and I couldn't wake her up when I went over to her house. I am so scared right now! Please! Hurry up and get here!" She stressed as soon as he answered the phone.

"What?...Are you fucking serious? When did this shit happen? Is she good? I am on my way right now! What hospital did they take her too?" Vincent asked, fumbling over his words as the shocking news caught him off guard and he immediately began thinking the worse. *Allah!*

Please let her be alright! Inshallah! He prayed, rushing out of the house and climbing into the car.

"We're at Saint Francis Hospital. Please hurry and get here Vincent!" Heaven pleaded.

"I am on my way now! I will be there in ten-minutes. Everything is going to be alright so try to relax and stay positive okay? It's in Allah's hands and he won't let anything happen to her." He promised, trying to sound reassuring even though his heart was pounding hard inside of his chest and he never felt more scared in his life.

"Just hurry the fuck up, please!" Heaven urged, hanging up the phone and immediately began pacing again as she waited for someone to update her about Miracle's condition.

Doctors were constantly to and fro out of the waiting room area conferring with other patient's relatives, but no one had yet spoke to her in regards to the well-being of Miracle and it started irking her nerves to the point that she was ready to flip the fuck out on everybody. *Someone better tell a bitch something soon or I am gonna go the fuck postal inside of here! Mark my mother fucking words!* She swore to herself and was about to press the nurse again at the station, until she seen Vincent rushing down the hallway towards her. There was a look of panic on his face as he raced quickly down the hall, weaving through the traffic of personnel standing about and embraced her in his arms. She felt grateful he had arrived because she was close to losing her mind.

"What's going on? Did you hear anything yet about how's she doing?" Vincent asked. But before she had the chance to respond a Doctor wearing blue surgical scrubs approached them and introduced himself. *About fucking time!* Heaven thought, trying to gauge the expression on his face as he stood solemnly before them. But she couldn't read through the neutrality of his disposition.

"Ms. Sanders? Hi! My name is doctor Evans and I am greatly sorry to inform you that Ms. Walters didn't make it. We've done everything we could to save her but there was nothing we were able to do, because she suffered extensive brain damage from the lack of oxygen to her brain..." Doctor Evan's had paused briefly allowing his words to sink in before he continued.

"-And, I am sorry to inform you that we were also unable to save the baby as well. So again, I am sorry for your lost." He sympathized with a slight nod of his head and casually walked away leaving them both standing in a dazed state of shock. *Oh my fucking God! No!* Heaven thought with anguish, feeling as though she was about to faint and had to grasp onto Vincent's shoulder to steady herself.

"No! This shit can't be fucking true!" She bemoaned in a state of denial because the situation was too hard for her to accept as Vincent wrapped his arms around her and couldn't believe that he not only lost Miracle, but also their child as well. A child he had no idea she was pregnant with until now and wondered why she never told him. *What the fuck! You stupid ass nigga!* He thought, feeling the heavy burden of responsibility for their deaths and knew he would never be the same again.

"She was having my baby!" He breathed in a small whispering voice as they both held tightly onto one another and mourned the death of the one person they had no intentions on ever hurting. But love was a notoriously fickle thing and mysterious in its own nature.

KQ
KINGS AND QUEENS PUBLICATIONS
Twisted
TREASURES
JC PIPKIN

MORE BOOKS BY
JC PIPKIN

www.ingramcontent.com/pod-product-compliance
Lightning Source LLC
Chambersburg PA
CBHW071247150726
48001CB00018B/330